I0535580

GHOSTWRITER

Terry Birchwood

If you've purchased this book without a cover, you should be aware this book may have been stolen property and reported as "unsold and destroyed" by the author. In such case the author has not received any payment for this "stripped" book.

The book is a work of fiction. All characters, names, places and incidents are the products of the author's imagination or are used fictitiously. Any resemblance to actual events, locales or persons, living or dead, is coincidental.

Copyright © JULY 2011 by Terry Birchwood

All rights reserved. No part of this book may be reproduced by any form or by any electronic means, including for information storage and retrieval systems, without written permission from the author, except by a reviewer who may quote brief passages in a review.

Publisher Sadie Books, 215 E Camden Ave H11, Moorestown, NJ 08057 → 856-313-0548

sadie-books.com

ISBN-10: 098-1604765
ISBN-13: 978-0981604763

Book Layout / Cover Design
C Allen Design – callendesign.com

ACKNOWLEDGMENTS:

The intangible Ruler of all people blesses me with the gift of imagination. I do not take lightly the privileges we have been gifted, the gift of thought is very powerful. And to that Power that keeps the rhythm of my life, I thank you for all. Thank you for the chance to experience the magic of life.

I also thank angels who support me on my journeys. Forgive any oversights.

Sylvester | Doshia | Russ | Marian | Agnes | Wendy | Tyrone | Candace | Michelle I | Armel | Ray | Cornelius | Andrew I | Scott | Vincent | Michelle II | Quentin | Richard | Marylou | Jody | Karen | Taryn | Madison | Andrew II | Christine | Inez | Harriet | Elizabeth | Yvonne | Arvilla | Clarel | Janet | Tracy | Charlie | Sherrie | Judy | Karen | Debra | Deborah | Lucy | Natasha | Kathy | Lula Mae | Maggie | Jill | Tyra | Sabina | Tom | Cathy | Alma | Annette | Cameron |

Thank you, reader, for taking a journey with me, outside of the box.

Terry Birchwood (aka Cass)

ONE - TABBY

"Between your legs, I take my feeding of juices so sweet and filled with nectar. As we roll on the grounds, our bodies wrap in tasty spaces. Sipping from your nipples, standing at attention, tapping on, and brushing, my hungry moist mouth. Hands reaching for warm places as sweet melodies escape our sexually charged voice boxes. Feeding on memories, so sweet, and equally possessed by your essence.

Ghostwriter"

I could not help but ache in that special place, as I read the email. Star had a way of making me feel as if she was wrapped around me at this instance. I imagined her breath on my neck as she moved in closer to deliver her soft lips on my shoulder. I felt her hands as she reached down to stroke my hips into a slow, seductive dance of passion. All I could do was throw my head back, reach behind me, and pull her closer to me.

Her scent became my air as she whispered sweet melodies into my ear. She slowly reached around to my stomach and lifted my skirt as if she were unfolding a precious gem with such gentleness, steadiness, and anticipation. Her hand found its way to my playground, pulsating and craving the touch of her warm fingers. She unfolded my soft skin and began to touch the moist mound that awaited her stroke. "You feel delicious."

The funny thing about Star's email, it was not directed to me. Star was working on a book and she would send me, what she called, snippets, from time to time. She claimed that she sent me sexual scenes to test if they were intense enough to get a rise in people. I once told her that it was difficult to get me sexually aroused through erotic novels.

She always said she would know if she is a good sex scene writer if I am moved by her words. So, I now read her words, testing my arousal thermostat. I cannot let Star know just how much her words aroused me.

I have been reading the snippets for years now. Star's words not only arouse me, but they tap my sexual gate, and leave me hungering, yet barely escaping, her gentle knock of authority.

Time to snap out of it. I need to get back to work. My partner will not understand how I could miss one of the most important deadlines of our careers because I was dreaming of an ex-lover.

What was I doing anyway? Oh, yes, call Sheila at Vertical.

"Hi Tom. It's Tabby. Is Sheila in?"

"Hey Tabby. Yes, Sheila is in, I'll get her for you. Please hold."

"Ok, thanks Tom."

"Anything for you, Tabby. Just a minute."

A few seconds is all it took for me to return to thoughts of my lover of long gone. Even though Star and I broke up a few years ago, she still moved me in a way where I wanted her to be a part of my life. Through the painful separation, we understood we were a part of each other's life. Star and I were together for one year; and it was such a rollercoaster ride of the most incredible experiences in my memory bank.

I wanted so badly to throw caution to the wind, go to her home, knock on the door, walk in, and begin a delicious tasting of each other, no words uttered. However, sense and sensibility had to stay in control.

"Hi Tabby. How are you? What can I do for you?"

Star, stay out of my head!

"Hi Sheila, I just wanted to check in to make sure the cups will be ready for the presentation on Friday".

"Yes Tabby. I already made arrangements for them to ship on Tuesday, and arrive Wednesday."

"You are absolutely the best. You know that Sheila, right?"

"I believe what you tell me. Tell me more", she laughed.

"No more for you Sheila, else your head will explode", I laughed at my own teasing. "Thanks for everything, Sheila. Are you coming to the brunch on Sunday?"

"As far as I know, unless some hunk comes along with a better plan".

"Sheila, you are too much, so freaky, horny, and so gullible".

"Uh oh, glass houses, Tabby!"

"Girl, you crazy. I've got to go. I have so much to do before Friday's meeting."

"Ok, check in before Sunday."

"Sounds good, hugs."

Where did the time go? I was famished and it was already one thirty in the afternoon. Bobbie usually packed me a lunch, but she had to run errands, so I was on my own. Star used to fill me with delights that she would personally deliver at lunchtime. She dropped everything to feed me at any time.

Star! Why can't I get you out of my head? I tried to conjure images of Bobbie sauntering in the room with a basket of delights, but those wishes were not answered. Instead, I saw Star's image in my head.

This had to stop. I was now married to Bobbie. Besides Star had gone on with her life. Even though she was not in an intimate relationship, she seemed to always be doing something with her business partner, Lexis.

Star always maintained that she and Lexis were not in a relationship, and they are just business partners. But I could see the way Lexis looked at her, as if Star were the prize of all prizes.

You see, Star vowed to never lie in bed with another, but to remain sacred for my return. At first, I did *not* take her seriously. And, then I took her *very* seriously, as time passed and she still had not bedded anyone. As more time passed, I began to feel uncomfortable, and I briefly thought Star might be obsessed.

When I questioned Star about her possible obsession with me, she replied, 'Tabby, I am not obsessed, I am possessed. But no worries, I have your best interests at heart, so this will remain my cross to bear. And, I'll never damage our friendship, possibly losing the last tie that binds us."

I was relieved when Star said she would not create conflict between Bobbie and me. At the same time, I was a little saddened. Star was so interesting, and different from most people. Oh, how I miss this woman, but that is between my thoughts and God. I am married now, and I will honor my marriage.

Plus, I love Bobbie! She is such a great mate. I met Bobbie two years after breaking up with Star. I was dancing the night away with David, and I felt a tap on my shoulder.

"Excuse me, did you drop this?" Bobbie held my purple cashmere scarf in her hand. I noticed her soft hands and my eyes ran up her arm to connect with a brilliant smile, accented by sparkling eyes. In the midst of getting my dance on, I froze in the sea of Bobbie's eyes.

"Thanks, um, you are…"

"Bobbie. The name is Bobbie."

"Is that short for something?"

"No. Just Bobbie."

"Thanks Bobbie, my name is Tabitha, but my friends call me Tabby".

"Well Tabitha, I hope you find time for a dance later."

"I have to thank you, somehow. A dance is the least I can do."

"And what else can you do?"

"Excuse me."

"I mean, can you sing, play an instrument, or act. I know, silly humor."

"It's not silly," I smiled. "It's just a unique approach. Do you want to know my zodiac sign, too?"

"No, then I won't have anything to talk about when we go on a date."

"Oh, a date!"

"It's worth a try. You know the club scene, if you don't take chances, the chance may be gone when you turn around."

"True, true", I said. "Well, Bobbie, should I be gone when you turn around, here is my number. This way, you can call me when you are ready for that dance, if we don't get to have it tonight."

Bobbie's smile flashed. I was interested in getting to know a little more about the woman behind that smile, if she returned for a dance or called me at a later time.

"Well, Tabitha…"

"Call me, Tabby"

"Well, Tabby, until we dance."

"Until we dance, Bobbie. Thanks again for the scarf."

"Look diva, get those feet going", David piped in. "Let's rock this!"

And so, David and I began to twirl again, sipping cocktails and bumping people back to jockey for space on the dance floor.

TWO - TABBY

"I invite you to invest in this breakthrough technology. Once complete, Webcepts' apps will revolutionize the way the world designs sites for business and home use."

The meeting group applauded. Now, it was up to OFE's board of directors to buy into the project.

I imagined going to the bank, with Charles, to deposit the investor's certified check. And then we would leave the bank, return coolly to the car, get inside the car, and scream with happiness!

A ten million dollar investment from one company was more than we ever expected. I remembered when Charles told me about the phone call that put this meeting in motion. "This is Richard Watson, of OFE. We like the SSS business plan. Show us why we should write a check for ten million dollars. Does Friday at noon in my office work for the presentation?"

I was thanking God that it was Friday. The presentation was finally over. I could relax, knowing I put every ounce of me into it. Now, it was up to OFE's board of directors to buy into the project.

"Great job, Tabitha. You make it very difficult to decline this lucrative opportunity. You will hear from us next week."

"Mr. Watson. Thanks for coming. Call with any questions. Ms. Peterson and Mr. Guilds, have a great weekend."

"Call me Richard. You will hear from us soon, Tabitha."

"Call me Tabby."

And with that, the visitors were gone. As Charles and I cleaned up the conference room, we discussed the good things that would come out of expanding partnership.

Charles and I have the solid experience, knowledge, and now the financial backing to pull this off. We spent the last ten years planning for this day basically from when we met at college.

Charles and I became very good friends, at college. Early on, Charles confessed he doted on me, however I immediately let him know we had the same taste in sex. Initially awkward, Charles smiled and replied, "Well then, maybe you can help me get a taste." We both laughed at his humor and the true friendship began.

During college years, Charles was a good-looking guy, but oversized glasses masked his good looks. It did not help that his wardrobe was too short for his tall, and lanky, frame.

Things changed over the years as Charles grew into his body. Women could not stop ogling him. Charles loved the attention. He saw no reason to settle down when so many women were clawing at him. There was no sense of desperation or urgency to get one. And Charles never seemed to feel lucky when the most gorgeous women would go out with him. Charles felt the women were the lucky ones.

He never let women spend the night at his apartment. He often said, " once they spend a night, they want a drawer in my bedroom, a shelf in my bathroom, a key to my pad, and my ring around her finger."

"I don't know how Bobbie got you to put her ring on your finger. I thought that was it for women, after Star."

"I am not a shifter, Charles. I love pussy. Always have. Some pussy is good. Some pussy is bad. But I still love pussy."

"You *are crazy*, Tabby. Absolutely crazy."

"On a another note, we are close to funding Webcepts. This will be so amazing and it's happening faster than I thought it could."

"We have a great service to offer, Tabby. I would invest the money, too, if I had it."

"Now we will have it, Charles."

After chatting with Charles, rolling back and forth between personal and business affairs, I decided to take the rest of the day off. We had done enough to secure the company for the next five years. Next week, we would know if enough *was* enough for OFE.

I checked my email before I left for the day. Hmm. Bobbie sends me kisses. I love her. David says don't be late for the brunch on Sunday. Oh, and there's an email from Star about the book.

"The motion around you had ceased, I gave in to you. I watched your lips as your eyes penetrated my flesh. If only I could take you down now, and lick the inside folds of your sweet pussy as you squirm beneath me. It would be fantastic.

Ghostwriter"

Not bad, Star, not bad. When I read her words, I felt like she and I were caught in those words. It didn't really matter, though.

I am happily married to sweet Bobbie, who gives me everything a person could want, and then more. Bobbie is loving, gorgeous, kind, and she holds it down. Bobbie is responsible and responsive to me as an individual. I love Bobbie. I love Bobbie.

It was time to get out of the office. It was beautiful outside. A walk down a few park blocks would do me some good, before I caught a taxi. The fresh air would clear my head of Star.

I love Bobbie. I am not sure what I'm feeling for Star, but I know I think of her, too much. I love Bobbie.

THREE - STAR

"Hi Lexis."

"Hey Star. What's up?"

"Did the new machines come in today?"

"Yup. And they are already in place, being used by some clients."

"Perfect, Lexis. Thanks. Is everything else good with the business and you?"

"Yup."

"Oh, and is the center opening in California on schedule as expected?"

"So far, so good."

Ok, thanks Lexis. Later."

"Later, Star. You are welcome."

I knew I was so lucky to have such a great business partner. Lexis was the best in the business. She had exceptional education and knowledge to run a fitness center, with or without me.

I remembered the day I first met Lexis. Tabby had a problem with her because of Lexis's strong beauty and intellect. Tabby could be very jealous.

Tabby always thought I was having affairs. Of course, I thought this was ridiculous, but what can you do? Tabby was protective. She was a lion protecting her den. I would tell her that she should be very happy that someone was looking at me because it showed she had taste.

Even though a few years have passed since Tabby and I broke up, I still cannot get over her. I was working to push her out of my head, all of the time. I constantly saw her smile, lips, and eyes. I felt her flesh. I felt her eyes on me. I smelled her sweet scent.

I fight these feelings and thoughts of Tabby. And I don't sit around moping. I date. But, I refuse to bring any to my bedroom. Women are initially drawn to the challenge of trying to have sex in my bed.

I haven't met anyone that I want in my bed, anyone that I want to see when I wake up. It is my most trusted place, where I rest my body and soul, where my most protected thoughts roam free, where I give of myself completely to a lover. I have not wanted to wake up to anyone since Tabby.

Yes, I have incredible sex with women. We meet, date, and have good times. And then they reach a point where "It's cool, I understand, we are just bene friends" becomes "I need to know where this is going, now". And that is when I say, "I know where I'm going. Bye."

I met a nice lady a few weeks ago. We were physically attracted to each other from the gate. I offered a drink to her, while at a bar for a quick after-work drink. She accepted, we chatted, and exchanged numbers. We went on a few dates. We had great sex, with the understanding that there were no strings attached. She agreed to the terms.

Four weeks into our dating, she wanted to take it to the next level. Four weeks! People will get together after a few weeks, and then spend months trying to get away from each other. I reminded this beauty of our talk, on where we stood with dating, and we continued to date for three more weeks. She decided she could not do this any longer because she wanted more. Bye.

So, while I date, I don't get too serious. I keep myself occupied with work, friends, family, and my current hobby, writing.

I really need to get back to writing. I was drawn to write a book, so I went for it even though I never wrote a book before. The writing process is really helping me to deal with my feelings for Tabby. It allows me to write about her without expressing any words directly to her.

I can imagine she may have wondered if I am trying to tell her something. I think of her when I send her the sexual scenes. It allows me to write with such intensity as it comes from a true place. Each time she states, 'You are still a great sex scene writer', I imagine shooting a sex scene with her – no cameras rolling, just us in our bed.

"I stared into her deep eyes, which seemed to pull me toward her. As I took steps across the room, with two cocktails in hand, I handed one to her. She reached for the glass and a little liquid spilled out the top. She licked my fingers as the brandy slid down them. As she licked my fingers, I let go of her glass. Now with a free hand, I touched her face, stroking behind her ear until a moan escaped her lips. She stood erect as I pulled her into me so that I could now lick the brandy off her tongue. I slowly licked from the back of her tongue toward the tip, as I inhaled her sweet, sweet scent. Hmmm, that tastes good. I held her waist with my free hand as I fed her a drop of spirits from my glass. She licked her lips and leaned up. I took her tongue in my mouth, slowly licking the ripples of her mouth. I felt her press closer to me with the intense heat of our playgrounds meeting in the middle. I kissed her lips and moved my tongue to her neck, just below her ear. I kissed her ear as if I were touching a precious flower petal, gently and magical. I pulled away from her and placed my glass on the table. I moved back to her and I placed my hands on her waist. I squeezed my hands a little as if checking a loaf of bread for freshness. I pulled her into me. She lifted her glass to my lips and I swiped her finger with my tongue as her glass met my mouth.

Ghostwriter"

Ok, I think that's good. And, I hit the SEND button. I was looking forward to getting a response from Tabby. I hoped that her vagina would jump when she read this.

FOUR - STAR

I cannot believe it is already Sunday. What time is the brunch? Sam said she had a big announcement for everyone. It could be anything with Sam. She lived on whims – whatever came to mind, she did it. Maybe she is heading out of the country, or getting married to her next husband, or opening a new business, or buying a zoo. Who knows?

Sam is Tabby's sister and I have known her for as long as I know Tabby. Sam was with Tabby the day we met in a grocery store.

Tabby and I were browsing the same aisle and we literally bumped into each other. When I turned to apologize to her, my heart increased in size. I was so taken by Tabby that everything around us froze.

I stared into her glorious eyes and asked, "Are you okay? I am so sorry."

"No problem. I wasn't looking either." After the world started moving again for me, I apologized for a second time and kept it moving. I could smell the woman that just seemed to transfer a love bug to me with a simple bump. She mesmerized me. I felt as if that bump was the beginning of a new seed inside of me. I felt oddly refreshed even though I was thinking about how tired I was before the bump. Hmm. I need to get this nonsense out of my head. I must be tired, really tired. I was single, and loving it. I had no time for thinking about ridiculous 'happily ever after love'.

So, I continued to shop, and was able to focus on the task at hand. While I was comparing salad dressings to each other someone said, "Tabby, don't forget to get the fat-free one for me."

Tabby. That was a new name for me. I smelled the woman who bumped into me. I looked to the voice sounds and the woman with the hypnotic aroma was smiling at me. "Sam, I did not forget about the fat-free." Tabby held on to the shopping cart, while her eyes held on to me.

Today, I wondered if her eyes would hold on to me at Sam's brunch. I took a shower, dressed, and drove over to Café Gallery. We liked to meet there, in big groups, favoring the charm, and privacy afforded to larger groups. I think a dozen or so people were coming; I don't remember.

Upon arriving at the Café Gallery, upstairs, I heard Sam's laugh, so I followed her voice. "Hey!!! Sam!!! How are you? You look gorgeous! My goodness."

"Thanks Star!! Need I tell you the same?"

"Yes, please, tell me", I laughed.

"You look gorgeous, too!! Well, you know everyone so get comfortable."

I walked around the table and gave a round of brief, heartfelt hugs and kisses to the circle. There was Sam, her best friend Tilly, her mom and dad, her brother Jonathan, Sam's arm piece Chad, Chad's dad and mom, Sheila and David were there, and a few more of Sam's friends. There were still a handful of empty seats. This must be *some* news because her entire family was at the table. Well, almost.

Tabby had not arrived. Oh, and Bobbie.

FIVE - TABBY

"...She lifted her glass to my lips and I swiped her finger with my tongue as her glass met my mouth.

Ghostwriter"

Hmmm. Star was at it again. My lips parted as I read the end of the snippet. I imagined Star pressed against me, taking me by the waist and gently parting my thighs with her leg. I imagined her 'inhaling my aroma', as she called it. I could see a cherry between her fingers as she slowly directed it to my mouth. I parted my lips more and took the cherry. The first bite, and juice splashed in my mouth. Star tasted my lips. I responded by releasing the cherry to her and following it into her mouth.

I loved Star's hot passionate tongue inside of my mouth. Her tongue seemed to say, 'I love you'. My tongue tingled when she touched it. I had never felt this way before, or after, kissing Star. I convinced myself this did not mean I was still in love with her. She was just the greatest love to ever mingle with me. She loved my body as if though God gave her the code to satisfy my sexual desires. I loved every moment she touched me. She knew when to be gentle and when to be rough.

And she had this way of getting me aroused until I felt like I had to take her inside of me so I wouldn't go insane. Her fingers would tangle with my gates until I unlocked the door for her to enter me. She visits areas inside of me that I didn't know existed.

I climaxed so hard with her that I thought I would lose my entire self, unable to return to normal day living. Any time Star took me, I forgot about everything.

"Honey, do you want your eggs scrambled or fried this morning?"

"Fried, Bobbie, thanks."

"Fried, it is."

Damn me. Bobbie. Bobbie. Bobbie. I love Bobbie and I am comfortable with her. I feel safe. I trust her not to break my heart.

With Bobbie, I gave my love, but I know I am a little damaged, incapable of accepting her love on level it had been offered. I was content, but not ablaze with love like I had been with Star.

A part of me shut down when I broke up with Star, the part that kept me from having my heart broken again, incapable of completely giving myself to another person, knowing that my heart could, once again, be shattered. Picking up the glass was not easy for me.

"Breakfast is ready."

"Ok, honey, I'll be right there."

As usual, breakfast looked and smelled divine. Eggs, toast, turkey sausage, grits, orange juice, tea, the works were on the table. Bobbie was a great cook, making it easy to open Café Gallery when the right financial opportunity came along. Bobbie loved cooking and she worked in the restaurant field since she remembered having a job.

"Sam is really excited to meet at the Gallery this weekend. I can't imagine what she has to say that she wants a gathering to hear the news."

"Tab, you know your sister is always in the limelight or some kind of light."

"Yes, I know my sister. Maybe you want to catch a movie Saturday since we're free."

"Pick whatever you want to see, my love."

"Whatever?"

"Whatever."

"Ok, I want to see the new one with Halle Berry and Julia Roberts, um, 'Just a Little More'. That looks good."

"Is it sappy?"

"What do you mean, 'is it sappy'? I thought I could pick whatever I want."

"You can. I just want to know if I should bring you some Kleenexes."

As I chatted with Bobbie, we met that quiet moment that tends to come in talk. I drifted to thinking about how I need to focus on my career. I needed to stop getting caught up in emotional nonsense.

I had come a long way from when I started a business with Charles. We got jobs from all over campus helping people with web design projects. We were known around the area for being able to custom design web sites, utilities, and apps, in record time.

We were soon able to put away money, even as we paid our college tuition and expenses. Charles and I began to realize we were onto something with this business.

Today, we are in a great position to build a powerful company by taking SSS to another level of business.

Focus on work.

SIX - TABBY

Sunday was here and I was going to be in the same room as Bobbie and Star. I tried to avoid being with both of them at the same time even though we were all cool, as people call it.

Bobbie was not insecure around Star. Once I caught Bobbie looking at me when I was looking at Star, but Bobbie never brought it up. She was good like that.

When we saw Star, it was in public settings. It was never the three of us, unless we ran into her at a function and that was short lived, 'hi, is all well, have a good day'. Star could overtake me with words, so can you imagine what seeing her could do to me?

Star was my hot sauce. She is so spicy; she adds flavor to whatever she touches, burns a little, but in a sweet way, that keeps you hungering for more of that hot sauce. That is my Star. I mean, 'that *was* Star'.

"Hey sis. Sorry, we ran a little late."

"Heck, fifteen minutes late. That's good for you honey!"

"Hey, are you bashing me before I even have a chance to get bashed?"

"Uh, oh", Bobbie piped in. "This could get ugly. Hey Sam. You look great."

Bobbie and I made the rounds, giving hugs and kisses to everyone. I knew Star was here. I felt her presence before I entered the restaurant. I had to keep control of this magnetism. As Star and I briefly hugged and said hello, I wanted to fall inside of her, and slide down to my knees as she parted her legs to signal my takeover of her. "You look good Star. How is everything?"

"Everything is everything. You and Bobbie looking good too." I waited for Bobbie catch up to me since Star was the last person to say hello to at the table.

"Hey Bobbie. It's been a while. You are looking good, as always."

"Thanks Star. It's good to see you. How are things for you?"

"Things are things", laughed Star.

Star was always using the same word to describe itself. She had such an elusive way of speaking.

"Well, let's toast, now that everyone is here. Thanks to you, my closest family and friends, for coming. To all of you."

Sam toasted in the air. Bobbie and I quickly grabbed the two glasses in front of us, at the two empty seats next to Star. We all raised the glasses."

"Cheers."

After drinking from the glasses in front of us, it would be awkward to move to another seat, so Bobbie and I found our selves sitting, with me in the middle of the two. *Control. Control. Control. I can do this.*

I could feel Star's body heat even though our legs were at least a foot apart. I imagined her taking her hand and resting it on my knee, and then slowly moving her hand half way up my thigh. I imagined her keeping up with the conversation, at the table, as if she had not just tapped my passion. She was excellent at engaging with other people; she gave each person the appearance he or she was the only one in the room.

"Hi, my name is Heather. I will be your waitress for the afternoon. Can I get either of you something to drink?"

"Club soda with lemon for me."

"Mimosa for me. Thanks."

I remembered when Star poured drops of Mimosa over my breasts. And she licked around my nipples, tasting the juice. I stood there, puzzled at the feeling. I felt as if she was my magic kingdom. That girl could do anything to me and it felt incredible. She nibbled at my breasts as she moaned lovely words, "So tender, so sweet, so delicious, so scrumptious, fill my mouth, satisfy me."

"Is everybody ready to get some food? Let's do this." Sam was the first to rise and she headed downstairs to the large buffet. I quickly followed her. I could see her give me the 'eye' as we picked our first round of goodies. I said nothing, but she knew what my return look meant, 'Don't go there!'

I grabbed some eggs, bacon, a bagel, some fruit, and a piece of French toast. I got back to my seat first. I knew Bobbie would be a while because she always took her time picking food. On top of this, she would be reviewing the food from every angle of a businesswoman, making sure that her employees delivered exceptional service.

There might even be a conversation with a staff member, or two, questioning the taste of something, or the presentation; one never knew what Bobbie would notice that seemed off her signature style.

I felt Star's heat as she approached her seat. As she sat down, she brushed my leg. It felt so good. I felt her heat transform into my body. I was on fire with desire for her. She apologized for brushing me. "Not a problem. So really, how are things?"

"Things are good, Tabby. You look more beautiful than I last saw you."

"Tabby, you know I am still mad at you for standing me up Friday night" piped in David as he took his seat.

"I know David, and I promised to make it up to you. I had all intentions of meeting you, but I did not realize how exhausted I was after preparing for that meeting. I could barely get my shoes off to get in bed. I had no energy. I probably would have fallen on the dance floor, or up the stairs, trying to get in the bar."

"Alright, diva. You're off the hook, but we dance twice next week."

"Ok, twice in the same night. I can handle that boo."

"Oh we are cute tonight, huh?"

"Every night darling."

"Hey David, what ever happened to Paul?"

"He was an absolute mess, Sam. Always talking, too much talking for me."

"Everyone gets on your nerves, quickly, or so it seems."

"Look Sam. I am open to finding the right one, but I won't force it if it doesn't fit."

"I hear that!" acknowledged Tilly.

"Me too", said mom as she glazed over at dad. After 35 years, mom and dad had such love between them, it could not go unnoticed. Their eyes twinkled when they looked at each other. It was if though they had the secret to love and passion. They often gave each other tender kisses in public, held hands, laughed aloud, were silly like children, and very concerned with each other's well being.

It was magical to watch. As I stared at my parents, I could feel Bobbie's leg rub my leg under the table. I felt uncomfortable, thinking Star would see this and feel some kind of way. Star made it clear she still loved me, that I possessed her. I never wanted to hurt Star's feelings. But heck, I am married to Bobbie. I would be a fool to hide my feelings for my spouse to appease an ex beau.

SEVEN - RICHARD

"I have a reservation for Richard Watson."

"Yes, come this way."

My dad and I made our way to our table and sat down. "As I was saying, dad, SSS is on to something great. We will be fools not to invest in this company. Over time, once we gain their trust, and offer them things unimaginable, they will let their guard down. That is when we will take over, and control the global web market."

"Richie, are you sure you are not missing anything with this deal? Ten million dollars is a lot of money."

"Dad, trust me. I know this business. SSS is the hottest company on the market right now. With the right partners, this company can grow to be worth hundreds of millions of dollars. The software prototype and presentation that I saw on Friday revealed possibilities I never imagined. Charles and Tabby have a plan to make it happen. They have been in the business for ten years and they already earn a few million dollars each year with very little overhead. They are genius at making money, keeping ahead of the market, and making people believe they want whatever SSS is selling."

"Ok, son. I'm going to trust you."

"Dad, if I mess this up, I will personally repay every penny to OFE."

You're that sure. Huh?"

"Yep, you bet."

"Well then, let's move on. How are Georgie and the kids?"

"Everyone is doing their best. Of course, Georgie is still sore over finding a woman's phone number in my pants. I don't even remember how it got there."

"I told you, son, you must respect your wife and never let her see your mess."

"Dad, I cleaned it up. I told her that it must have gotten picked up with other papers at the office. It must belong to someone else."

"And you think she bought that nonsense."

"It doesn't matter whether she bought it. It matters that she stops talking about it."

"Oh, is that right? Is that what you learned from me? Richie, I always respect your mother. I make sure I do NOTHING to hurt her. Do you understand? She carried my children, took care of me, raised my family. There's no room for disrespect. Do you understand me?"

"I understand."

"Hello gentlemen, can I get you a drink?" Thank goodness for the waiter because I was not in the mood for my dad's crap.

"Double scotch on the rocks. Thanks."

"A gin giblet for me."

"Your waiter will be over shortly, to take your orders."

EIGHT - TABBY

I was so at odds around Star. I daydreamed of reaching out and touching her thigh. I loved to rest my hand on her thigh when I sat next to her. It was my way of saying, "I am always here with you."

I could see her chest move up and down as she slowly recycled the air in front of her. I saw my finger slowly going down the center of her pants as the back of my hand brushed the inside of her legs. I felt the heat between her legs and her breathing increased in speed. I saw her eyes close as her head went back, the sigh of delight escaping her succulent lips.

"Is everyone having a good time?"

'Yes' we all said.

"I am glad. Well, you all know I asked you to come here to share some news."

"Sam, spill it."

"I'm pregnant."

Silence and shock swept the room, quickly followed by 'oh my God', 'congratulations', 'I cant believe it', and 'I am so happy for you'. Everyone was smiling and raising glasses to toast.

"And before you ask, Chad *is* the father. Oh, and we are getting married."

"What? I mean, Sam, this is a lot to absorb", shrieked dad. Dad was the quiet one of the bunch, so when he exclaimed something, eyes turned and ears listened.

"Well, I mean, congratulations dear. Are you sure you know what you're doing?"

"Father, I love Chad and we were already talking about marriage before I found out I was pregnant. We are just doing things a little out of order", smiled Sam. Sam hung onto dad's every word. Sam always wanted to please dad. What he thought about everything she did meant the world to her. Dad was Sam's special person. She and mom loved each other, but she was always more comfortable hanging out with dad.

Sam was a tomboy so she wanted to do everything dad did, when we were growing up. They fished together, fixed cars, watched sports, all the things people expect a dad and son to do together. I am sure Sam held a special place in dad's heart because of the tomboy bonds. I was not jealous and I did not want to trade places with Sam. I hated sports, fixing cars, and fishing, until I met Star.

How in the hell did I get back to Star? Please get out of my head.

"Hey Bobbie, can you pass the Splenda. Thanks, honey."

Questions and answers flew around the table. 'Is it a boy or girl, where are you getting married, how long were you engaged, is it going to be a big wedding, and on and on. Everyone at the table appeared genuinely happy for Sam.

Even though this would be her fourth husband, Sam always went into her marriages with a hundred percent of her heart. The first two marriages did not work out. The first one cheated with Sam's best friend at the time. The second one became emotionally abusive. The third husband died from pulmonary heart disease.

I did not imagine Sam would marry again. We always talked about the baseball rule, 'Three strikes and that's it. We are out of the game." Well it looks like Sam is coming out of retirement.

"I would like to make a toast. To the beautiful bride-to-be and her fiancé, Chad. May you both enjoy each other's love for as long as you desire."

"Here's to the engaged couple."

"Cheers."

"To Sam and Chad."

When Star lifted her glass, her shirt twisted so her breast was revealed. I imagined her breasts brushing on me as she pulled me in her arms for a taste of her tongue. Her tongue was always so sweet. I wanted to take her tongue into my mouth and tango with it, right now.

I wanted to push her down on a bed and slowly climb on top of her. I wanted to sit on her well-crafted member and take it all inside of me as I arched my back to make room for her. I wanted to feel our strides mesh beyond our comprehension. I wanted to get lost in Star's delight.

I continued to nurse some desserts – strawberries and brownies with whipped cream. This was a good distraction for me, something to look at so as not to be tempted to glance at Star. I imagined her sitting on the table in front of me, pulling me onto the table as she moved my dessert to the side. I saw her lay on top of me and make love to me through my clothes. I felt our soft fabrics move with our hunger. I tasted a strawberry, tickling my tongue with juices. I felt Star's tongue inside my mouth. I saw her open the buttons of my blouse. I felt her warm hands brush my bra's fabric, connecting with the nipples under Victoria's Secret underwear.

"Well, I hate to eat and run, but I have to get some work done for a big meeting."

"Really Star, so soon?"

"You know you are spoiled, Sam. I have been here for two hours and you know that is a long time for me to be anywhere."

"This is true, you are always on the go, since you..."

Sam grew silent, as I sent her a telepathic glare. *Star's been on the go, since what Sam? Since what, Sam?*

"I mean since you moved into the new place and---."

"Yea, I have been busy since then."

I felt like Star and I could read each other's minds, and told each other to remain cool. We knew Sam was talking about since we broke up! Sam did okay avoiding saying this, but she still touched close to an awkward and haunting topic.

I was haunted by Star. I thought of her in every free space. I hungered for her. I forgot about Bobbie when thinking of Star. I wanted to taste Star. I wanted Star to taste me. God, please help me release these thoughts! I am married, and faithful.

I took an oath to have and to hold until death do us part. I did say I would be faithful and I am faithful to my feelings for Bobbie. It is the feelings for Star to which I have been unfaithful. To live with an imaginary life in one's head and not follow the dream is to not live one's life. Or is it something like 'do not let the heart control the mind.'

Who am I fooling? I can sit here, thinking of one thousand clichés and references to support being with Star and being with Bobbie. I can see trying to juggle both of them, but I cannot see lying to either of them. I am not a liar.

"Well, everyone, I'll be off. It's been a true pleasure being in your company. I love you and wish you a great evening." Star made her rounds, starting away from me.

As Star passed around the table, Tilly piped in, "I had better get going too."

"Another one. Uh oh, I think this party might be over."

"No girl, I am staying", David chirped as he put away another Belgium waffle.

"And you know we have to talk about the wedding", chimed in her mom.

Chad's parents, Hanna and Paul, were quiet. I had never met them before this afternoon. I noticed their English was not very good, so this was probably why they kept a low profile. And with all of us talking at the same time, and using slang at a mile per minute, they were probably lost.

It looked like only Tilly and Star would be leaving on the first departure bus. I was tired, but I knew that I could not leave at the same time as Star. I was afraid I would look like I only came to see Star. Lord, help me calm down. I was a wee bit paranoid.

NINE - STAR

I had to get away from the Café. Being near Tabby was quite difficult for me, even though on the surface, I am sure I did not appear affected by her presence.

I got high just at the thought of her. Being near her was like being near my favorite food on the other side of a fence. I could smell her, almost taste and feel her. But I could not touch her.

Matters were made worse by the fact that Bobbie owned the restaurant. I was in their company and their space; my feelings were overwhelming me, right now.

The air on my face was refreshing; the slight wind eased the anguish. I felt free again. I headed over to one of my favorite bars, Zeke's, to grab a beer.

"What's up Zeke?"

"It all good, Star. What's up with you?"

"I'm cool. You know me. The usual, hon."

"Here you go."

"Thanks." I left Zeke a hefty tip and made my way to the jukebox. I had no song in mind to play; I just wanted to poke around to pass time.

Three beers later, I made my way home. I daydreamed of Tabby the whole while. I remembered our exchanges in the front seats of this very car. I remember when she said, "Star, touch right here" while I stared ahead to concentrate on the road.

Even though she was cool in posture, her nipple was incredibly hard. She was an expert at prolonging sexual climax, building to a state that seemed never-ending.

I always wanted her, now, earlier, right now, and now. After all these years in her presence, I thought this would fade away.

I can't take this anymore. "Hi Tabby".

What am I doing? My stupid, stupid ass called Tabby.

"Hey Star, what's up? Is everything ok?"

Ghostwriter , Terry Birchwood

"Tabby? Oh sorry, I hit your number by accident. You are right next to Terry in my phone list."

"Aha, Terry. How is he? We didn't get to catch up at brunch."

"He's good. He's good. Terry is still whoring, and still cute. Anyway sorry to bother you Tabby, take care."

"Oh no, no bother. I was just settling down on the couch with a glass of wine."

"Well then, if memory still serves me, I am sure Bobbie would like some private time with you and that wine, Tabby."

"Actually, Bobbie is still at the restaurant. You know how dedicated she is to her job. She won't be home until sundown."

"Oh, so you have some time to yourself. That is good too."

"Yes, that is good." A silence took over the space, and I could hear Tabby breathing. I could see her cleavage rising and falling, her moist skin luring me closer. I could smell the sweetness of the wine and the perfume surrounding her flesh.

"Well, I apologize again, Tabby." Enjoy the rest of your Sunday."

"Ok, Star. Thanks, you too. I…"

"I'm sorry, I didn't hear you."

"I… am glad you are doing well."

"It's all good. You know me. Right back at you. Bye, Tabby."

I had to hang up that phone. The sound of her voice lulled me to places I work so hard to not visit. I might be a little tipsy, but I know I cannot tell Tabby I called her on purpose and I savor her. I love her too much to add confusion to her life by luring her to commit sexual acts with me. I want her when she is ready.

TEN - STAR

I had a busy day so I would not soak in Tabby's essence all day. I am into this woman in ways I did not know anyone could be into another person. Yes, I have it bad. I feel her with me, I see her smile, and I hear her giggle. She is stamped on me.

I still cannot believe we've been apart for so many years. The first day apart, with me in a hotel, after being told to 'just go', I thought, 'once she cools off then...' The next day, I thought 'well, she is really upset'. More days passed and I realized I was up the creek without a paddle.

Something got fucked up, along the way and I could not put my finger on it. She said she could not believe what I had done. I tried to find out what she was talking about. The more I asked, the madder she got until her anger mixed with disgust.

Well, she is gone now, so I must keep working to move on. Let's see, ten thirty with Johnnie, two o'clock with Marvin. I had time to check on MyBody and get a little paperwork done. I need to check in with

Lexis anyway. She will want to know how I plan to handle Marvin since he'll be getting his second pink slip.

"What's up, sunshine?"

"We seem to be. What are you doing in so early, Star?"

"I have a couple of appointments today, and I wanted to get a few things done before I head off for the day. Plus I wanted to see you and discuss Marvin."

"Oh yea, Marvin. You know this going to be his second warning."

"Yup. I am going to speak with him this afternoon and put this to rest, one way or another. You know I will handle it."

"You always do." Lexis stared in my eyes a moment too long and I felt uncomfortable. I looked away.

"You know, I think the new machines are working out well. I see a lot of people starting their routine with them and people always seem to be using them. We may have to invest in a few more, but we'll decide that after a couple of months."

"Sounds good to me, Star."

"Cool. I'm going to get a few things done, and get outta here."

"Ok, Star. Let me know if you want or need anything." Something about that *anything*' put me in an uncomfortable state again.

Lexis made it clear she would tangle with me if I were interested in dancing. After a few attempted shakedowns in earlier days, she stopped dropping innuendos. Maybe I was reading too much into this.

I needed to clean my keyboard. It was a mess, with dust and remnants of meals come and gone. I remembered when Tabby placed her hands across my vision while typing on this same keyboard.

"Guess who brought din-din?"

"Hmm. Let's see. Is it the pizza man?"

"It better not be!"

I turned my chair around and grabbed her into my lap. I moved in for a kiss. Tabby did not resist. She opened her lips ever so slightly so my tongue could continue to part them. Tabby uttered a soft, "Yes".

I ran my hand around the back of her neck and pulled her deeper into my mouth. She lingered with me as I took a breath between kisses to savor the delectability of this. I could see the sun glistening off her cheek. And, I saw the mesmeric shadows between her legs.

Tab was wearing a red mini skirt with black tights. The tights had a hole directly in the center of the crotch. I fingered her through her soft panties. I would touch the tip of her clitoris, gently nudge in, and then pull out. I played with the inside of her thighs. Tabby opened and closed her legs as she quivered, responding to my touch.

I felt so much with Tabby. I felt warm air sweep through my body as if music was playing on my very flesh. Tabby was my symphony and the music sounded great.

Tabby stood up, abruptly, and just stared at me. Her eyes seemed to say, "I love you". I could feel it.

Tabby walked over to the window and then stared ahead for a few moments. Then she turned around and came back to me. She sat on top of me this time, with a leg placed on each side of me.

I pulled her into me and I could feel her breasts brushing my chin. I loved to rest my chin in her soft cleavage. This place was so succulent and cozy.

I could feel her clitoris throbbing beneath the layer of fabric that separated me from her playground. I nudged at her panties, as if I were about to rip them off. Then, I let go. I rubbed my face on Tabby's face. She meshed into me so perfectly.

Tabby began to slowly make circular motions on top of me. She did the dance of passion. I reached inside her blouse and loosened the bottom snap of her bra. Her breasts made a bounce and showed off themselves more.

I heard the whispers escape my lips, *Tabby*! I could not be completely silent with Tabby. Tab knew how to take me to states of bliss where I wept aloud.

I placed my hand inside Tabby's bra and began to make circular motions on her nipple. That soft spot hardened as I nudged at it, gently pinched it, held on steadfast, and released it. I took turns seducing each nipple with the one hand, while the other hand grabbed her ass, pulling her forward and down at the same time.

Tabby answered my knock for pleasure by riding me. She threw her head back and wrapped her legs tighter on the sides of my legs. I wanted to fall on the floor with her. I kept my wits about me and focused on savoring every moment.

I placed my hand in Tabby's panties and felt the soft wetness of her folds. I stroked just within her folds, being careful not to penetrate her. I circled the area, stroked up and down, squeezed, and simply rested my hand just outside of the magical entry. Tabby moaned so loud, I knew people in the fitness area must have heard her.

We cared not what was heard, said, or seen. We only saw each other. I brought my hand up to my mouth and tasted her sweetness…

"Hey Star. Jonathan is on the line."

Johnnie, some damned timing!

"Ok put him through for me. Thanks Jeff."

ELEVEN - TABBY

Star had me hooked on her passion. I lay there anticipating her. I arched my back to receive her. She penetrated me with such confidence and gentle command. Just as quickly, she pulled out. My lips trembled, as my vagina shuddered.

"Hey sweetie. It's time to get up. Hey. You need to get yourself going, now honey. Remember, you're meeting OFE peeps for breakfast today."

"Mmm. Hi sweetie. Thanks. I am so tired."

Bobbie kissed my forehead. She was so gentle and thoughtful. I felt so guilty that I was still trembling from Star's touch, no matter that I dreamed the encounter. It felt so real.

"Are you okay? You seem a little cold."

"Cold? Oh, I guess I just woke up and might be a little chilly. Whew. I guess I am. I'm going to catch a warm shower and I'll be down in a minute. Thanks again, love. I could have slept all day."

"Anything for you, Tabby. You my boo. That's what we do. And, I would do you, if you had time."

"There'll be time to do me, later."

Bobbie was a good lover to me. She was thoughtful, and a little shy, which made her adorable. I reached climaxes with Bobbie, but not as powerful as those I reached with Star. I knew what to expect from Bobbie. She would kiss me for a while and move her hands around my body. Her hands were warm and I felt comfortable.

She would move down, caress my breasts, feed on my special area, and finger me a while until I would climax. When I tried to nurture her body, she clammed up, saying, "I am fine. Pleasing you pleases me." Soon, I stopped trying, but I still enjoyed cradling with her." She was safe.

The shower felt good. I tried to wash Star from my body but instead I imagined that her naked body stepped in the shower, behind me. I saw her flesh begin to get wet as the water hit her on all places. Her penetrating eyes swept my skin as if she was caught in a trance. I rubbed soap on her breasts and across her stomach. Star took the soap from me and rubbed it on my shoulders. Things began to get very slippery to the touch in that shower.

"A few more minutes!"

"I'm coming honey. Almost done!"

Okay, snap out of it. I had better get my ass in gear. Charles and I were, soon, to find out just how much of a partner OFE cared to be, once we got to Hot Bunnies. The food is great there, as if mom cooked.

I got dressed, scented up, accessorized, and I was downstairs in fifteen minutes. "You look spectacular."

"Thanks Bobbie."

"Really, you are ravishing. You get hotter all the time. I don't know how you do what you do, but I like it."

"You like it. What's it?"

"All of it", she smiled sheepishly. When Bobbie smiled, I felt like a kid. She has such a pure, simple way about her. I felt young again, and safe.

"This is a nerve-wracking day. God, help me get through this day."

"Babe. You know you are the best at what you do. There is no reason for OFE to reject the bid *they* put on the table. Remember you didn't seek them out. They found you."

"I know, I know."

"Well, then. Get out there and bring home that big slab of bacon."

I kissed Bobbie softly on the lips. I held her eyes for a moment, thinking about how wonderful she is, and how I don't deserve her love. But I was content, and I felt safe.

"Mmm, I hope there's more of that when I see you tonight."

"It depends on how the meeting goes."

"Well I can cheer you up, or we can celebrate. Either one will involve those lips. I love you, Tabby."

"I love you back."

TWELVE - TABBY

The ride to Hot Bunnies seemed to take days. I was going over my presentation, again and again. *How was my posture, did I seem confident, did I sweat?* I knew I was being ridiculous. I was the best in the business; well … Charles and I were, are, the best in the business.

Everyone was waiting when I got there, Richard, Charles, and two other people that I didn't recognize. "Hello Tabby. You are as beautiful as ever."

"Richard, is that the good news before the bad news?" We all laughed.

"Can I get you a drink?"

"Yes, a glass of orange juice. Thanks. So, how is everybody? Ready for some really good food?"

"I am famished. Hi Tabby," said Charles. He was impeccable, looking like he was on top of the world. He was dashing and smelled of sweet cigar. Looks like he was already celebrating something today. Charles only smoked cigars when he felt a momentous wave in life.

"Tabby, before we get to the point of this meeting, let us enjoy breaking bread with each other."

"That works for me. Oh my apologies, you are…" I looked at the other two people who had come with Richard.

"Henry Daisley, I am OFE's Vice President of Operations. I'm pleased to meet you. I have heard wonderful things about SSS."

"And,"

"Yes, of course. Ralph Evans, Vice President of Software Strategies. My pleasure."

"The pleasure is also mine."

"Well, then gentlemen, let's toast to a great breakfast." Charles knew how to keep the energy casual, without losing the focus of the business. "And we shall also toast to the potential for great business."

Glasses bumped and turned up. "What do you like here, Tabby?"

"The French toast is divine. Oh, and the eggs benedict is wonderful too. Actually, everything is delicious that I've tasted. And I have been around the menu."

"Are you all ready to order?" We made the rounds, *I'll have this and that and can you make this like that and can you leave that on the side and take that off?*

The waiter was perfect in delivery. Everyone enjoyed the meals. "Tabby, you were right. This food is great. I am stuffed and feel like taking a nap. Well, maybe I'll do that after we do business."

"I am listening, Richard."

"To get to the point. We like what you have to offer. We want to sign the deal based on everything set forth in the contract, with minor changes."

"That's fantastic news," Charles did not break a sweat or miss a beat.

"We believe SSS is on to the greatest development project to come along in a while, and we would be fools not to invest, looking at the potential return."

"And your board of directors, did they raise any concerns?"

"Nothing out of the ordinary. Nothing that couldn't be addressed internally, thanks to your great presentation last Friday."

I nodded and smiled a cool smile. "Richard, I am thrilled with the news. How do you want to proceed?"

THIRTEEN - RICHARD

"Dad, it's done. We signed the deal."

"Very good, son."

"Based on my plan, we should nip away at that percentage in a year. Can you hold a minute, dad?"

"Hey babe, I am on the line with my dad, can I call you right back?

"We need to talk, now, Richie."

"Look, I can't talk with you right now. I said my dad is on the other line."

"Dad, sorry about that. We should be able to make a hundred times our investment in the first three years. And if we---"

"Hey son, did I tell you that YOU TALK TOO FUCKING MUCH! We will talk about this in person, only! Understand?"

Yes, I understood that my dad has issues. He was always complaining, no matter what I did. It could be fucking annoying at times.

FOURTEEN - SAM

I almost went into shock when I learned I was pregnant. Thirty-five years old, I had given up the thought of bearing children. I never got pregnant before, so why now? This must be a sign from God that Chad is absolutely the one and it will work with us.

When I started getting tummy aches, I thought I was getting food poisoning. Two missing periods later, and a few pounds heavier, I knew something was not as usual. Dr. Kim confirmed that 'something' was going to be a 'someone'.

And, I thanked God for my family and friends to help me get through. Tabby was there for me through everything. Even though we sassed each other, what seemed like, all of the time, we had each other's backs through everything. Tabby wiped my tears, yelled me out of bed, and told me this would be great. Tabby was there.

I wish Tabby could be there for Star. I know it's none of my business, but I saw the way they looked at each other at brunch. After all these years apart, they still shine within each other's company.

Yes, I was shocked when I first found out Tabby liked women, but I loved my sister. I wanted her happy, and I never saw her happier than with Star. They rode each other's waves so well, they laughed, cried, argued, and most of all they loved through it all, until that night Tabby shut down.

Tabby often told me, 'If Star messes this up. That is it. I am done with love.'

Tabby said Star messed it up, but I still wonder what really happened. Star never told her side of the story. I know she tried to talk to Tabby, but Tabby would not listen. I suppose Star felt if it did not matter to Tabby, fuck everybody else.

I don't think I will ever forget the night they broke up. Tabby came over one night, in an unusually silent mood. We had fluffy chitchat about work, dating, and *what is life all about?* After a few minutes of enjoying the sounds around us, Tabby pulled a letter from her pocketbook. She handed it to me.

"Hello Tabitha. I'll just get to the point. I am Star's mistress. I know it will be hard for you to believe this so here are a few things that only a lover should know about Star. I can tell you, her private cell phone number is 555-424-8787. She has a tattoo of your two fingers on her left ass cheek. She barely sleeps because you snore, but she won't tell you this even though she hates it. I bet she said she was 'going to take you to her bed, where no woman goes'. Didn't she? Get out while you can, Tabitha. It's better you find out this way, than through catching her with me, or possibly someone else. I love Star more than life, and I am sure I love her more than you do. I hope you can step aside and let us continue our bad romance. Do you love her enough to let her be with me like I let her be with you? Move on to something better, Tabitha. You are too good for her. I am perfect for her.

The Other Lady Fucking Star"

I was stunned. I did not know what to say to Tabby. "Tabby, this can't be true" was all I could muster.

"Can't be true! Look what she knows! Tattoo of me, private cell phone number! It's fucking true and it's fucking over!"

"Tabby, what if it is not true? You have to talk with Star."

"Talk my ass! It is so fucking over between us! How could this bitch know these all of things about us?"

I didn't know what to say. I had no answer.

"Just as I thought. No answer. It is fucking over, FUCKING OVER!"

FIFTEEN - STAR

I still had twenty minutes to kill before meeting Johnnie at The Continental Diner. I knew he would be on time. He was always on time. Paperwork and email was under control. Lexis was holding down MyBody, and I could take a deep breath. I kicked my feet up on my desk for a moment.

I remember the first time Tabby and I were at the diner. We ordered pancakes. I got blueberry, and she got chocolate. We split them on each other's plates. I asked for a full can of whipped cream and made it clear I would pay for it. I squeezed some on one of my fingers, and, little by little, I licked it off as I stared into Tabby's eyes.

I could feel the elderly woman, at the next table, eying me with a horrified stare. I chuckled and suddenly blew her a kiss. Her glass of water rattled, on the table, as she quickly turned away. I had no shame. I was terribly smitten.

I had known Tabby for three months. I loved her company. I was feeling things I had never thought existed. Up until now,

Ghostwriter | Tony Birchwood

my claim to fame was as a gigolo, a hot lover with no commitments. With Tabby, I could only think about commitments – how committed I was to not missing a date, making sure I touched her whenever I got close enough, savoring every moment with her, and soaring with no fear.

I tossed a little whipped cream at Tabby. She laughed and wiped it off her cheek, well most of it. She reached over, as if to put her finger in my mouth. When I opened my mouth to receive her, she swiped the cream across my neck.

"I will clean that up later."

"Oh really."

I looked at Tabby as if to say, "Clean it up." She smiled and took a bite of her pancakes.

Lexis brought me back to earth. "Hey Star. Don't you have to get going?"

"Thanks Lexis. See you tomorrow. Call if you need anything."

I was only two minutes, walking, from the diner. I was hugging my brother in no time.

"Hey Mr. Man. It's good to see you. You look great. How is everything?"

"You know, Star, I can't begin to tell you how crazy I am at the office. I will just say, at least it is paying off in the salary. That's why I wanted to meet you. I want to talk to you about work. I got offered a huge promotion; actually it's a really, really huge promotion. Hundreds of thousands of dollars in yearly increase, my own car, big office, travel opportunities, what I always wanted."

"That is excellent, Johnnie. Have you told Erica the great news?

"That's just it. I told Erica."

"And?"

"Well the new opportunity also comes with moving to China for three years."

"China! Are you serious?"

"This is not joke material, Star. Of course, I am serious. This is what I always dreamed of doing. Erica is not feeling this and I don't want to lose her. Her family is here, and she's having a tough time imagining being so far away from them. I get that, but I also get that I need to follow my path."

"Well, if you move, your family will be far away from you too. With the money you would be making, Erica could fly back to the states any time she wanted."

"I know, I know, but this is my dream, not hers. And, stop calling me Johnnie; it's Jonathan now."

"Ok, Johnnie. So what are you going to do? Have you decided? Gosh I am so happy for you. Whether you take the job or not, there is proof you are the man! My lil' bro' got it goin' on!"

Speaking of the devil." Johnnie excused himself and took a call from Erica.

"Tell her 'hi' for me."

SIXTEEN - CHAD

I am going to be a father. I still cannot believe I am going to be a father! I am only twenty-eight and this is not what I had planned. I wanted to spend a few years enjoying life without the responsibility of little people on my shoulders. How was I going to be a dad? I am only twenty-eight!

Ok, calm down. You love Sam and she is carrying your child. You should be happy. This woman is carrying YOUR seed! Thirty-five years into her life, with no children, and she was carrying your seed. You should be honored. Okay, okay, I'm okay.

I am not sure what mom and dad think of this. Mom smiled, cuddled me and said, "Wow, son." Dad just looked at me and said "ah mi hijo de dios". There was no emotion on his face. I knew they were a little shocked, and I understood this – a baby and a wife. And, Sam was not the race they had hoped.

Well, it is what it is. I am going to be a husband and a father. Okay, I had to pull it together. There's no time for wallowing in my own anxiety and fear.

I was doing Sam a favor and picking up Tabby from Hot Bunnies so she could come over to help Sam with the baby shower and wedding stuff.

The ride to Hot Bunnies did not take long, and Tabby was already waiting outside.

"Hey, Chad." I gave her a hug.

"Thanks for this."

"Sure Tabby. How is the business coming?"

"Well, I will just say, things are looking up", Tabby let out a huge grin.

"OFE bought in? OFE bought in? OFE bought in!" Tabby nodded her head in excitement. "Wow! That is incredible!"

"I am still in shock."

"Tabby, this is great. Let's stop at Gino's and pick up a bottle of wine."

"Cool. Oh no, Sam should not drink, so let's not tempt her."

"Oh, that's right, I am going to be a father. Tabby, I AM GOING TO BE A FATHER!" I began to smile from a place that told me everything was going to be okay. I just imagined that little head nestled in my hand, with the rest of it tucked away in my arms like a football. I have to be so careful holding MY baby. I am going to be a father!

"Chad, I know we had, and will *have* our ups and downs, but know that I love you because Sam loves you. If you ever hurt her, I will kick your ass. And if I can't kick your ass, I will hire someone who will kick you're a…"

"I get it. I get it. You know I love Sam."

"I know."

We sat in silence for the rest of the ride. Tabby looked out the window and hummed some tune that I never did make out. It seemed like she was a million miles away.

The Ghostwriter | Terry Birchwood

We rode the rest of the way in silence while I thought about my new roles as a dad and husband. I am getting married! Ay dios mio!

SEVENTEEN - TABBY

As Chad and I sat in silence, I drifted off to a time when Star and I spent the weekend with my sister and her previous boyfriend, Timothy. Our apartment was being painted so we decided to take stay with family for the two days. Sam and Timmy, as I called him, decided they were going to see a movie that I didn't want to see. Star stayed behind with me.

Star and I lit a fire and talked. We had wine and apple pie with French vanilla whipped cream. As we talked and treated our palates to sweets, I began to feel as if we had transported to a land of love, peace, and perfection. That very moment, I felt I could die and have no complaints, as I could not imagine a life that could get better.

Star talked about the evolution of man. She spoke of the Erectus, and was fascinated by the jump from a species four-foot tail to one creating tools, weapons, fire, and learning to cook. She felt divine intervention was behind humankind's development, even as she had no ounce of proof.

I remember Star wondering how kissing and sex evolved. She said, "I wonder how I would have kissed you and made love to you, had I lived ten thousand years ago."

"That is a very interesting idea."

"Hmm, well we are here now."

"And."

"Where are we sleeping anyway?"

"In the basement suite."

"Hmm."

"Oh no."

"Oh no what."

"You know what."

"I know what."

Before I could respond, Star was touching my neck. She knew I loved her hands on my neck. Her hands were warm, soft, and I always felt fully caressed even though she used one hand. Any touch from her filled me. I got goose bumps, warm feelings, and I felt super happy. I know this is corny, but I now know what crazy love is all about. I am crazy for Star.

Star reached over to touch me, and she spilled her drink. "Uh oh", she laughed. "I think we have some cleaning up to do."

I raced to the kitchen to get napkins. Star giggled and followed me. "Get the napkins, quick!" Star taunted.

I grabbed a couple of napkins and turned to leave the kitchen. Star blocked my path, and she pulled me into her. I put my arms around her neck. She responded by pushing me up against the refrigerator and then she began to unbutton my jeans. I surrendered as I leaned on the refrigerator for balance.

Just before I was about to melt into my memory of Star, I heard Chad say, "Well, Sam will be glad to see I got you here in one piece. She says my driving sucks!"

Laughing, I said, "Chad, she don't like my driving either! Funny thing is, I think she is the bad driver!"

"You and me both." We laughed at our little tag team on Sam.

"Ok, Tabby, I will catch up with you two in a few. I forgot to pick up Sam's cleaners' clothing. Let her know I'll be back as soon as I can. Oh and I may stop at Stu's for deli stuff; I've been having the taste for it."

"Sure, Chad. I'll tell her. See you soon. Thanks again, sweetie."

"You're welcome. Okay, later, Tabby."

EIGHTEEN - STAR

After meeting Johnnie for breakfast, I took care of some business at the bank and post office, since I had a little over an hour to kill before meeting Marvin.

I had asked Marvin to meet me at Judy's Place so we could talk outside of work. Judy's Place is a great restaurant a few blocks from the office. When I got there, it was only one-forty so I ordered a beer at the bar, and reserved a table for two.

I nursed my beer, and my mind drifted to a time when Tabby and I met at a bar and pretended we didn't know each other. We decided we would take on the roles of two people out on the prowl, looking for a good time, and only a good time.

I arrived first and sat at the bar. About twenty minutes into chilling at the bar, I noticed Tabby next to me dressed in a tight black dress, with red shoes and a thick red belt surrounding her delicate waist.

"Great shoes", I said.

"Thanks."

"Star, the name is Star."

"Well, thanks Star. Here's to great shoes." Next, Tabby tapped my beer bottle with her glass of water.

"To great shoes."

"Oh, I'm Tabby."

"Tabby. Lovely. Short for Tabitha?"

"Yes. Good guess. Impressive."

"I am not good at the pickup lines, so I'll be brief. I think you are gorgeous and I can't stop imagining your red shoes in bed with us. I know this can go any way. It can lead to submission, a tease, or a dismissal, but I am taking the risk because I don't want you to leave here without knowing I want to taste you."

"I see. Well, Star, right? I submit." She leaned over and licked my lips with an unhurried gesture. I closed my eyes, and enjoyed the gesture.

Just before I was about to follow my daydreams out of the bar and to the hotel we went to, I heard Marvin say, "Star. I am sorry I'm late. I got stuck in traffic."

"You're late?" I looked at my watch. "Oh, ten minutes late. Wow, I didn't notice. Anyway, how are you Marvin?"

"Good. Good."

"Let's get our table."

We made our way to a cozy corner away from the main crowd. I wanted a quiet spot so Marvin and I could hear each other.

"Well before we enjoy a great meal, let's just cut to the chase. Rumor has it around the center you are touching some clients in ways that some see as inappropriate. Is this true, Marvin?"

"I don't know what to say. I'm shocked."

"Well, two clients said you had a hard-on while training them, and you brushed up against them a couple of times. Given your past experiences trying to date clients, I am inclined to follow up with you to make sure we don't have a problem here."

"Tabby, with all due respect. My penis is huge. I doubt if they saw me hard and the clothing we wear *is* revealing."

"Yes, the clothing does fit tightly. And no disrespect to you Marvin, I have seen your crotch and I get your point." I could not help but laugh. "I understand how this might be a problem for some of our clients. I will stress, *some*."

"I can't win for trying."

"Marvin, I came here to put rumor to rest. I think it is ready to sleep. We can solve this; try jock straps. You can stand to make your tees a little longer, too. Try the Papi Cotton Stretch straps; they are comfortable and soft on the t-bone."

"I won't ask how you know that. So, we cool, Star?"

"It's all good, Marvin. Let's eat."

NINETEEN - STAR

I was in the mood to go home and relax after meeting with Marvin. I turned on my computer and worked on Ghostwriter for a little while.

I penned some delicious sex scenes in the process. I ran across a passage that I thought would move Tabby. Just when I was about to hit the SEND button, I thought maybe I should stop sending book snippets to Tabby.

I gave Tab my word that I would do nothing to upset the balance of her marriage. I haven't done anything, but I know my sex scenes are written to her. If she can feel the truth behind the fiction, I am affecting the dynamics of her relationship with Bobbie.

Okay, I will stop sending snippets to Tabby. I will stop sending snippets to Tabby. I will stop sending snippets to Tabby. I must stop sending snippets to Tabby! Okay. Stop.

I wanted a distraction, right now. Working on the book was getting me worked up, so I decided to go to Yetta's. The music would be good and the drinks would be strong. Plus, I could walk there.

I cleaned myself up and walked to Yetta's. There were about fifty or so people at the bar so it was a nice sized crowd.

"Hey Stefan. How's it going?"

"Wonderful, and you diva?"

"It's good. Let me get a Ward Eight."

"Fierce choice, coming right up."

As I spun my finger around the rim of the glass, I listened to Usher, on the jukebox. I couldn't help but start singing along with him, *"Wifey home, wedding band, I'm a lucky man. You'd think I'd be satisfied and truthfully, yes I am..."*

"Sorry to interrupt the singing, but can you pass me those chips?"

I looked around and saw a sinfully delicious woman. I knew that she was addressing me because her eyes were all over me.

"Sure no problem."

"Thanks, um, you are."

"Star's the name."

"Interesting Star. I am Heather."

"Nice to meet you, Heather."

"Likewise. So, do you have a wifey at home and a wedding band? I didn't notice one on your finger but that doesn't mean you don't have one somewhere."

"I don't have a wifey at home and I don't have a band." I lifted my finger.

"Whoa. Watch where you point that finger." Heather smiled and pretended to hover to protect herself from my finger."

"It won't hurt you, I promise."

"Oh, that's disappointing."

I was a little surprised by her comment. Heather made it obvious she was at least flirting, if nothing else.

Ghostwriter | Terry Birchwood

"Do you want it to hurt?"

"Sometimes, just a little bit, but hurt and feel good at the same time. The feeling that can come with breaking new barriers or ground, you know."

"Wow, you are really thinking this out. Intense, are you?" I laughed at Heather's direct approach.

"Well, I have to talk it out because I want to fuck you. I am rationalizing as to why I should or should not fuck you. I am wondering if you will be a satisfying lover."

"Whoa, just get to the point huh." I was intrigued by her forward approach.

"Why not get to the point? It's not a bad thing. We understand each other's intention from the gate. Makes for a faster lane to yes or no. Why waste time with smoke and mirrors? I know what I want so I get to it."

"Your take on it is refreshing and actually, I prefer the candor from the gate. So tell me, would I get to fuck you as well? I think you are quite fuckable, Heather."

"Actually, I don't like it up the ass."

"I said 'as well', not 'ass'."

"I heard you. There is a huge penis under this skirt, Star. And I want to fuck you with it. I said I like to get to the point so here's another point. I am a transvestite and I think you are mouth-watering."

"You shittin' me Heather."

"No shit, baby. I love women's clothing and I love taking on women's mannerisms, but I love pussy even more."

"Well, again your honesty is very refreshing. It's better that I find out about the penis now than later. While I still think you're hot, I am not feeling the dick right now. No hard feelings, right? No pun intended."

"No hard feelings. Hey Stefan, whatever Star orders tonight, put it on my tab."

"Okay, baby."

"And Star, the invitation is always open."

"You are sweet Heather. One never knows what the future will bring."

"You can say that again. Have a double lovely, diva."

And with that Heather was gone.

TWENTY - BOBBIE

"Richie, you know I wouldn't call you unless it was really important. I can't believe you got so upset and nasty!"

"Look, Bobbie, I *am* sorry about that. I know I was a little nasty, but it's been a busy week. Do you forgive me?"

Richie pulled roses from behind his back, and a box from his jacket pocket. The emerald cut diamond Eternity ring, staring at me from the box, did it for me, all fourteen of those diamonds.

"My sweet, look at all of the precious items I continue to stock for you. I cannot believe Tabby has not caught on to you yet. Four years into the relationship? She must be blind, stupid or both!"

"Can I get some of the credit? You know I hate that bitch, so I work hard to make sure I destroy her, no matter what it takes. If it means being a lesbian for a few years to make sure she is taken down, then, so be it, I am a lesbian."

"Frankly, I still can't believe you hate this woman so much. But, I hope you continue to hate her so we can pull this off."

"How can I not hate her? I lost everything because of her. And why would she know? Surgery can do many, many things to alter appearances, and it's been over ten years since that bitch ruined my life. I've grown a lot since then, in many ways."

"Well Hell. At the least, you would think that *ex-lover* of hers would sense something."

"She is too busy hiding her own 'something' or so she thinks. *Everyone* knows she still loves Tabby. It's fucking pathetic!"

"Ok, don't get all riled up. You still haven't told me. Why did you want me to hang up the phone on my dad to you talk to you?"

"Well, the urgency is gone now. Since you couldn't talk, I had to make a decision."

"Decision on what, Bobbie?"

"Well, Tabby is floating on air because of this deal she signed with OFE. She wants to protect the money, just in case something happens to her. She mentioned willing me her portion of the company, and we decided to talk about it when we got home.

I wanted to talk to you to make sure I made the right decision. I know getting a portion, should something happen to her is great, but I don't want to leave any trails that could haunt us later, either. You know the deal, I am going to fuck her up."

"So, did Tabby make a decision?"

"Yes, she changed her will the next day and willed everything to me. Of course, when we talked about it, I did not get excited and I even asked her to make sure this is what she wants to do. I reminded her that I have my own money, and don't need it."

"Hmm, that's interesting. This is brilliant. So whatever she has left becomes yours, if she should – um – die?"

"You got it. Well, if she dies or I divorce her ass! Whichever one comes first. I hate that bitch!"

"I know, but be patient. You put in four years already, one or two more will seem like nothing."

"Don't worry, I've come too far to fuck this up. I want her destroyed."

"You are the best, Bobbie. Come give daddy some of that lesbian love."

"I got your lesbian, fucker! You know I can't stay long, so make me come quick. I can use some dick, right now. Eating her pussy is getting exhausting and it tastes funny."

TWENTY-ONE - SAM

"In here!"

"Hey sis, how's the baby doing, boy or girl?"

"Too early to tell. My little sweetheart is still a glimmer in my eye, right now."

"Hell, Sam I can't be---"

"Uh, no more cursing, Tabby. The baby will hear you."

"Oops, I'm gonna need a book on this." We both laughed as I sat down next to Tabby."

"So, Tabby, tell me. How are you?"

"I'm fine. Why the strange look?"

"You know I love you right?"

"Oh shi---, I mean oh, shoot. I know you love me. What is following this?"

"I just worry about you Tab, that's all. I know things are over between you and Star, but I---"

"But you what? Actually, Sam, I really don't want to go here. Star and I were over years ago. I have let go and move on. Well, I have moved on. And talking about her with you will not allow me to let go."

"Where is this coming from, Tab? I haven't brought up Sam in over a year. Wait, you haven't let go, that means you still love her. I knew I wasn't crazy. You still love her! Don't you?"

"Don't get excited. I'm not sure if it is love, lust or what it is. I am possessed, just as Star. I know what she means, now. She has a piece of me even though I am living without her."

"Trust me. You have a piece of her too. I see the way you, both, look at each other without facing each other. I see the shifty eyes, the flame continuing to burn under the smothered coals."

"Oh really? You see all that! Humph!! For real? Really?"

"Come on, Tab, I know you. You're my sister for God's sake!"

"I don't know why I still desire that woman after she cheated on me and told me lies to woo me. Her mistress put her shit, I mean stuff, out there. She is lucky I still talk to her, however casual."

"But Tab, you never let her explain herself. How could you separate yourself from such love based on a letter?"

"Who else would know those things except someone intimate with her? Can you tell me that, Sam 'cause you sure couldn't tell me when I asked you back then?"

"Of course, I couldn't. I was just as shocked as you. Years have passed, Tab, which gave me time to break things apart. You know how I love to break things down. I thought, maybe this person who wrote this letter might not be Star's mistress. It could be someone right under your nose that would know this stuff. I don't know."

"Oh, that's very unlikely, sis. Thanks for clearing everything up. You need to work on plan for trying to fix things between Star and me. That was not convincing. And, did you forget? I am married! Okay, just leave my Bobbie and return to my cheating ex. Oh yeah, Sam. That's brilliant."

"Tab, I'm just saying, you have something with Star that I have rarely seen between two people. I don't see that magic when you are with Bobbie. I have never seen that magic with you and anyone, except Star. Look me in the eyes and tell me I am crazy. Here, right here, in the eyes, Tab. Come on, Tab, I'm just saying."

"And I am saying too, I cannot trust Star. I am married, in case you keep forgetting, Sam. Why are you trying to get me to cheat on Bobbie?"

"Okay, okay Tabby, I will leave this alone, for *now*. Mom is on her way so we can plan the baby shower and start thinking about the wedding, so let's swoop that drama out of the window. If mom gets to talking about this, we won't get anything done."

TWENTY-TWO - STAR

"Hey Star, I hope all is okay. I haven't received a snippet from you in a couple of months, which is unusual? Is the book finished? Hahaha!

Tabby"

Hmm. She is thinking about me. Tabby, huh. Sweet taboo is more like it. I've been doing such a great job at avoiding Tabby. I managed to control the urge to ghostwrite her for two months, one week, and four days, but who's counting? I still write emails; I just don't hit the SEND button. God, I miss her.

Fuck, I guess I should respond to her email. Ok, keeping it simple.

"Hi Tabby, thanks for checking in. I am doing okay. I am crazy busy getting ready for MyBody opening in California, so I haven't had much time to write. Heck, I've been working on this book for five years now; I guess adding a few more months to the project doesn't hurt since I have no deadline. Hahaha! I'll see you at Sam's baby shower. You know I can't miss that. That sister of yours! I love her. She's a great girl. Anyway, I've gotta run. I hope all is okay with you and Bobbie. Take care.

Star"

That's enough. Don't get carried away and write a damned novel.

Okay, pull it together. Lexis and I need to get to the airport in three hours. I called a car service and headed over to Lexis's apartment building. "Hey Lexis, I am on my way. I'll be there in twenty minutes."

"Cool. I'll be outside."

The ride was a little congested since it was mid-afternoon. There were the expected backups, pedestrian traffic, horns beeping, and eighteen-wheelers making deliveries all throughout the city.

Oh. I forgot to call Terry. "Hey Terry."

"Hey Stardust."

"I'm heading to pick up Lexis. Don't forget to check on my place every couple of days. Remember, we'll be gone for one week."

"I know, Stardust. We've done this a thousand times. I know the drill, diva."

"I know, Terry. Ok, I will stop acting like a granny nanny. Call if you need anything. Love ya dude."

"You too, Stardust. Have fun for me. Kiss."

Hmm. I was still stuck on the fact that Tabby is worried about me. She hopes I am okay. Hmm. Tabby, oh sweet Tab, I miss you. I wish you were going on this trip to California with me.

I got lost in my mind during the taxi ride. I remembered the last time Tab and I had traveled together. "Tabby, don't you just love this room?" I looked at the excitement on her face."

"It's perfect. I don't see why I need to leave. It's very cozy."

"For you, Tabby."

"And this is for you, Star."

Tabby walked to me and kissed my lips. I felt a warm sensation rush through my body, and I placed my hands at the bottom of her back. I felt Tabby's body calling me to nibble at it. I began to nibble at the left ear as I moved my right hand up to rub the side of her arm.

I felt her soft skin beneath the sheer fabric, which moved so easily across her skin. She breathed heatedly and I felt the warmth of her breath on my cheek. I licked at the corner of her mouth, in a teasing way. Tabby's mouth came forward, and I moved back a little. She opened her eyes and looked at me as if to dare me to tease her. I took the challenge.

I grabbed Tabby's hands, and held them firmly, but not enough to hurt her. I placed her hands behind her back and I leaned in to kiss her neck. I took both of her hands with one of my hands, as I unbuckled my belt. Tabby sighed with delight.

I fastened Tabby's hands with the belt; she put up just enough of a resistance to create more sexual energy between us. It got fierce, with high energy and hunger, in that room. Tabby stood in the middle of the hotel suite, staring at me.

I backed up, and I looked her up and down, slowly. I slowly unbuttoned my top, but I didn't take it off. I knew how much she loved when I wore leather bras, so I gave her a slow and steady show. I came close to Tabby, and I walked behind her.

I unzipped her top and let it fall down. The top settled near her waist since her tied arms would not allow it to fall free. I took my hand and began to stroke the middle of her back. She shivered.

"Is this close enough for you?"

The taxi driver sliced my sweet thoughts. "Ok. How long will you be ma'am?" I couldn't believe I was already at Lexis's place, already.

"No time. Just leave the meter running."

Lexis was only a few feet away. I got out of the taxi, gave her a hug, and helped her get her bags into the trunk.

"Thanks, Star. How was the ride?" Lexis and I settled in the taxi and I signaled the driver to continue to the airport.

"The usual, but could have been worse."

"Yea, remember last week when that four-car collision delayed traffic for *hours*! They really need better routes around here. It's getting so damned congested around here."

I laughed, "It's always been congested. You ready for Cali, Lexis? We're going to put MyBody all over the place."

"I wish you would."

"Now, now. No time for meow, Lexis. You know what I mean."

"Hey, a girl can dream. Anyway, you know I got over that, years ago. Just teasing a bit. I am just loosening up a little. Hell, we're going to Cali! Okay with you, Star? Can't a girl play a little as she heads to the sunny skies? Really!" Lexis shot me a grin.

"It's all good. I knew you were playing. I am just a better player."

"Aha! Is that a fact?"

"Check", I laughed at the silliness of our conversation. I settled back and closed my eyes since we had a while before getting to the airport. Lexis had on really high heels, like Tabby used to wear. Tabby, those legs of yours made me go yum. I thought of one of our encounters.

"Do you see these pumps, Star."

"Yes. Tabby."

"Do you know what they signify?"

"No, tell me Tabby."

"They represent me wanting you to fuck me. I want unbridled passion, ruled by your gentle heart and guided by your mighty sword. Got that?"

"Yes, Tabby."

I went on and on in my head, remembering the good times, which seemed to be all of the time. I never seemed to run out of good thoughts of Tabby.

Lexis chilled, too. She seemed to have her own daydreams going on. We both seemed a little surprised when we heard, "Shall I help you with your bags?" as our taxi driver put on the brakes.

"Ok, time for the next lap. Thanks, keep the change." Lexis and I did what we had to do to get from the taxi to the plane. What a week this was going to be for the two of us.

Lexis is the best in the business when it comes to developing plans to open a fitness center. I know she did everything to make this more fun than business. I never have to worry about anything being out of order because of Lexis.

"Let's do this, Tab--, I mean Lexis."

"Are you sure you are taking the right girl?" Lexis teased.

"Of course I am, Lexis, this is business."

"And, if it were pleasure?"

TWENTY-THREE - STAR

Everything is as it should be in the new MyBody. The building is complete, all equipment was in place, the key codes and alarms work. Most importantly, we've got over five hundred prepaid memberships.

We were having a pre-opening party for the staff. We told the staff members that each could bring two guests to the party, so we had quite an interesting crowd of people that evening.

I was mingling with staff and their guests when I got a little flustered. I excused myself and headed to get a bottle of water.

I was flustered at the view across the room, actually. It was Tabby. Even though I could not see her face, I recognized her hair and those red shoes! What a tease. I scoped the room for Bobbie, and saw no sign of her.

I played it cool and walked in Tabby's direction, while looking in another direction. As I neared her, I directed my glaze to her shoes. "Wow, Tabby! What a surprise." I could not help but smile.

The woman with the red shoes turned around to see whom I was talking to. The woman was not Tabby.

I was stunned, but kept my cool. "Oh my, I apologize, Ms. Um—"

"Shavon. You can call me Shavon. So. Tabby. Is that who you thought I was? Sorry to disappoint you. Your voice sounded so happy to see this Tabby."

"Oh, no problem. I just thought you were someone else." I shrugged it off, hoping she did not notice my face on the ground. I could not believe this was not Tabby, in those red shoes with that thick wavy curl.

"So, Shavon. What do you think of this place, this party?"

"I haven't been here long enough to make an opinion on the party, but the energy feels good, so far. And from what I can see, the interior colors are beautiful. Also, it's spacious and I love the light fixtures."

"Well, if you ever want some of those light fixtures, let me know, and I will hook you up. I know the owner."

"Really? Must be nice. I imagine you live around here too."

"Too. So you live around here?"

"Well, yes, Glaze, my sister—"

"Aah, Glaze is your sister. She's great."

"You know Glaze?"

"Small world. Anyway, I have taken enough of your time, Shavon. It's a pleasure to meet you."

"The pleasure is also my pleasure. Oh, I never got your name."

"Star, Star Duncan."

"Wait? You're the owner? Star?"

I smiled, "Yes, one of them. Let me know if you have any questions, more comments, or want to get a membership. And thanks for the feedback. I am happy you like the place from what you can see of it." I smiled.

"Oh, yes, I like the place and all it has to offer, from what I can see." Shavon stared at me in a way that penetrated me. It's as if she knew me. It was almost creepy.

I walked away, thinking, have I come face to face with a woman who truly intrigues me? Or was she just some semblance of Tabby that I would try to mold into more of a Tabby until I grew tired of her because she isn't Tabby?

TWENTY-FOUR - TABBY

I wished Bobbie and I could go to the grand opening of MyBody, but I know it's best I keep away from Star. As much as I want to celebrate her successes, it is not a good idea to mix so much because of my pull to her. I have a difficult enough time getting her out of my mind when I don't see her. When I see her, my soul and flesh pull strongly toward her.

In my mind, I want to converse to no end, laugh at all of life's miracles, challenge her intellect, run with her, and make love to her. Star has worked some things on me that defy any presuppositions. My desire for her touch is beyond reason or circumstance. It is strange land to be in, knowing I am not in a place to succumb to her pull.

I feel confident that Star intentionally pulls me through her emails, which I desperately miss. On the other hand, I hope she does not see the magic she works. I want to appear disinterested, over the relationship. I am married, for God's sake.

Hell! I wish I could go to the grand opening of MyBody in California and take Star's body and nestle it with *my* body. I could almost feel her soft hand go beneath my skirt as she pulled the skirt up enough to rub the inside of my thigh.

I remember just about everything when it comes to Star. It was the grand opening of the first MyBody. Star took me into an office and had a snack. She snacked on my neck, lips, and shoulders as her hand played with the inside of my thigh. A few minutes into her snack, she touched the tip of my clit and then she slowly let go of my skirt.

"Time to get this show started, Tabby. After you." And she led me toward the door as she slapped my ass one fierce time. At that moment, my vagina ached for her to charge in, but she did not, so much as, touch me again, as we left the office.

Star was so spontaneous, like the wind. I wanted to run with her, surround myself with her, have her inside of me, and snack on her.

Why is she not writing me? Is the book finished? Does she have a new playmate? Did I just say, playmate? God, help me through this.

Bobbie's voice helped me focus on now and stop this damned daydreaming, already.
"*Hey, Tabby!* There's a package from a Richard Watson at the door. It's for you."

"Richard? What's that about? I'm coming."

"Hmm. Richard? Huh. Is there something you want to tell me Tabby? Flowers, from Richard? *And*, a note?"

"Bobbie, you know who Richard is, so stop playing. You'd better get used to it. Flowers might start coming every day, Bobbie." She tickled me at the sides as she laughed at me jumping up and down to rid myself of her groping fingers. *What on earth could Richard want?*

"Hi Tabby.

Just sending congratulations on a job well done heading up this historic undertaking.

Keep up the great work. Give my best to Charles. Talk soon.

R. Watson"

The note was very nice. Richard and his dad, Nicholas, appeared to be pleased with the past few months. Things were going very well, very well indeed.

We already hired seventeen of the twenty-five new employees. The lease was paid up for five years. We had great financials, and soon we would be coding the most powerful web-design software ever released.

TWENTY-FIVE - TILLY

"I am so blessed to have you as a best friend, not only a best friend, but also a great business manager. Surely, you know how much you mean to me? Right?"

"Don't be silly, Sammie. What is all this sappy stuff anyway? That baby is making you mushy, huh?

"I guess so, Tilly. I never imagined that I would have a baby. I always saw myself as the strong woman, explorer, traveler, diva, free spirit—"

"Alright, alright, I get the message."

I laughed at Sam's self-introspection. It was nice to finally see Sam exuberant about something. Even though Sam was always the life of the party, the person that everyone invited to the party, it always seemed like something was missing in her spirit. That something looks like it was a baby because I don't see the empty space in her anymore.

Sammie seems alive in a way nothing else made her, not even Chad. I know that Sam loves Chad, but there's something about that marriage does not fit right with me.

Yes, Chad is charming; he is somewhat exotic, and he is very handsome. Yes, he treats Sam like his queen. But something behind that smoky stare, and half-tilted smile seems blank. I know I should mind my business, but this is my best friend. I need to do what best friends do, have each other's back, even if she gets mad at me for snooping behind her back.

Okay, what am I doing? I cannot ruin this for my Sammie. She is so happy. I am being ridiculous, overreacting. Heck, I need some rest.

Sammie snapped me out of reviewing her life's choices. "The red or the green one?"

"What, Sam?"

"Where are you, Til?"

"I'm here. I was just thinking about how you are going to make a very beautiful bride, Sammie!"

"You bet I am!'"

"So, have you and Chad already discussed finances and things?"

"Really, Til! You think I would marry a man and not know his financial status. Knock, knock! Hello, is Tilly there?"

"Ok, Sammie, just checking. You know that's what best friends do, look out for each other. I would *hope* you have my back, if I chose to get married."

"I know, sorry if I was being a bitch. Oops, I mean, witch. I am nervous with the baby, and the wedding. Add to that Tab's business expansion. SSS is growing so fast, I hope it doesn't spin into a tornado. You know what I mean?"

"Yea, but I think Tabby and Charles are the best in their business."

"Maybe they are the best in the business, but let's just hope they know how to *run* that business."

-130- Ghostwriter | Terry Birchwood

TWENTY-SIX - STAR

"Hey, Terry. Is everything good?"

"Yes, Stardust. Your home is still here, just as you left it. How about with you?"

"Things are good. MyBody's opening went off without a glitch. Thanks for watching my place Terry."

"Girl, please. If I don't do it, who will?"

"Well, I can't talk long. I just wanted to check in. Hugs to you, babe. I'll check back in a couple of days."

"No need. I will call if something comes up. Just do what you do, Stardust. Sprinkle your magic in California. Leave a blazing trail heading home. Ciao Bella."

"Mwah. Later, Terry."

Terry is such a good friend. I can't believe we have known each other for over twenty years. And who knew that young jock, chased by all the girls, only wanted a man in his arms.

We sure cannot judge books by the cover. I imagined him with a beautiful, statuesque woman. Who knew? Just shows that gender, sexuality, and behaviors blend in the most unique ways.

I wished Tabby were here with me. She was my beautiful, statuesque woman. I recalled a time I was getting ready for a trip that Tabby could not take with me. I was almost through the front door.

I had my luggage, identification, all of my travel essentials. I went through a mental checklist with Tabby – keys, check, wallet, check, credit cards, check, tickets, check, check, and check.

I reached over to kiss Tabby. The kiss was intended to be brief, but her lips were so scrumptious that I fed from them until the taxi driver beeped the horn for me to get my ass in gear.

Well, reality came after me. No trips for me with Tabby. We are done.

Lexis's voice helped me get back on task. "Star, are you ready? Why do I always beat you to the door?"

"Coming, Lexis."

"Let's go! We need to get going. We are running a little late."

"Coming, coming!"

Lexis and I headed to the California office to meet with the employees. We wanted to recap the first week of operation. Things went well. Staff offered great feedback, suggestions, questions, ideas, and more.

When the meeting was breaking up, I noticed Shavon through the meeting doors, sitting in the lobby. Wow! She is definitely breathtaking! I wanted to walk up to her, grab her hand and take her on a picnic. I had childlike thoughts, looking at her. She seemed refreshing.

While the meeting ended, I found myself next to her in the lobby, as everyone said their goodbyes. "So, you again, how are you Star?"

"It's all good. How about you Shavon?"

"I am good, too, Star."

"Hey sis, I see you met by boss, Star", Glaze joined in.

"Yup, Star and I met at the party."

"Oh yea, anyway, Star, I will be seeing you on Skype. Are you still heading back home after the weekend?"

"Yes, work to do, always. It's been great seeing you and meeting your sister. I will be in touch."

"Hey, Glaze, if Star doesn't mind, I will catch a ride with her. And you can take my car. Cool with you?"

"Wait, take your car, but---"

"Take it or leave it, both of you."

"I'm in", Glaze quickly added, looking at me with pleading eyes.

"Well, I guess I'm in too, unless—"

"Yes, unless?" Shavon looked deeply into my eyes.

"Unless you change your mind."

"I am not changing my mind."

Before Shavon's words were out of her mouth, Glaze was off and running to the car. She was pulling off, while Shavon was still looking deeply into my eyes. She looked at me, like a lover, like someone who knew me. It was chilling, yet intriguing, and eerily comforting for me.

"Star, what would you like to do? Pick anything, and I will do it with you?"

"It's that simple?"

"Yes, Star, it's that simple. Tell me what you want, and I will give it to you. Do you know what you want?"

"I want ice cream."

Lexis approached as I looked at Shavon. "Hi, Star, are you ready to go?"

"Hey Lexis. Meet Shavon, Glaze's sister."

"Yes, I remember seeing you at the pre-opening party. How are you?"

"I am well. It's nice to meet you."

"Ah, Lexis, I am going to give Shavon a ride home. You go ahead, and I will see you for dinner at the hotel."

"Oh. Ok, I'll see you tonight, Star. Don't be late for the dinner meeting. Okay, it's nice meeting you, Shavon."

Lexis disappeared as fast as she showed up.

"Then, let's go get some ice cream. Would you like me to drive?"

"Only, if you can drive well. If so, then feel free to have a go at it."

"I am an excellent driver, Star. I am a great passenger too. Rides can be thrilling."

"Oh, so you like rides?"

"Don't you, Star?"

"Sometimes", I responded.

We went for ice cream, and we got to know a little more about each other. I had a good time with her that day. She taunted me on and off. I played ignorant to the sexual innuendos. I asked questions about her life and aspirations. I shared the same.

During our pleasant conversation, I realized I was drawn to the echo of Tabby. Shavon and I did not have that much in common. I think we both realized this.

After a couple of hours shooting the breeze, we wrapped it up because I needed to get ready for the dinner meeting. We promised to keep in touch and get together when I was in California. And that was that.

TWENTY-SEVEN - TABBY

What the hell is going on with Star? I cannot imagine why she pulled away so abruptly. Yes, she says she's okay, but just busy. She has never been *too* busy, in the past, to write me. She's been back from California for a while.

I had to admit, I missed those snippets. I missed the tales that seemed dead-on to some things we had done together. Then, there were things she wrote that I wanted to experience with her, like her slipping her hand inside my playground as we go down the roller coaster. She had some crazy ass imagination. That's for sure.

Star knew what to write to burn a fantasy in my head. She knew how to write so the words transformed to visions in my head. I could almost, hear, feel, see, smell, and touch her. Star's words jumped off the computer screen and tickled my flesh.

I imagined her feeding on me. I sat on her prize as she took me from behind. I arched my back and leaned forward to hold on to the wall. My rhythm was slow, intent, working to satisfy my hunger for Seven. Yes, this was just the right size for me. I held on to my breast as Star held on to my waist. Star was on her knees, delivering passionate knocks within my playground. I felt Seven play with my inner walls and tap at the special place known only to us.

I felt Star's soft lips touch the center of my back as she moved as if to claim my pussy as her own. She fed me pleasure beyond my wildest dreams, as it got more and more difficult for me to hold on to that wall.

Star pulled me backward until I was on all fours. She maneuvered herself underneath me, while telling me to remain on all fours. It was all I could do not to fall down on all seven inches of her fuck pole and push Star into an orgasm. She touched my breasts with her moist lips and the heat of her tongue sent a tingle all over me. She looked up from those intense eyes and breathed in as if I were her air.

My knees buckled and I fell on top of her. Star took me into her arms and held me still. She took one hand and moved it to the side of my face, holding on enough for me to know she was there, but gentle enough so that I could move at will without feeling pressure of control exerted on me.

I let out a soft moan as the heat from Star's body surrounded me. I felt like I was caught up in a cloud of comfort and passion. Star moved beneath me as she pounced at my playground without entering. I would have taken her inside of me with one swift move, but she wanted me to wait for her time.

I looked down into Star's eyes and then pressed my face against her face. I felt her shiver. I delighted in her reaction to me.

Bobbie reminded me that I was now with her, and no longer with Star. "Hey, baby. Whatcha doing'?"

"Hey, sweet Bobbie, I'm just resting for a minute, and enjoying the time."

"Whatcha thinking about? Are you thinking about what I'm thinking about?" Bobbie winked at me and smiled that dear smile.

"It depends."

TWENTY-EIGHT - RICHARD

"Whoa! What in the fuck are you trying to do, Bobbie?"

"Hmm. You don't like that?"

"Like it? If you don't move your hand away from my ass, we are gonna have a problem. I think you've been spending too much time playing a lesbian. Are you still playing? Ain't no penetration going on here. If you want to lick my dick or balls, that's fine. But nothing going up my ass, you crazy bitch."

"Fuck you Richie!"

"That's your problem, Bobbie. You are not fucking me. I am fucking you. Turn over."

I reminded Bobbie why she let me fuck her every week. I fucked her until she looked like she was going to faint.

"Who's fucking you, Bobbie?"

"You, Richie, Ooohh, oooh, aah shit! Fuck me, Richie. Fuck me!"

TWENTY-NINE - STAR

"Star, what time are you coming? You *are* coming, right?"

"Are you *kidding* me? I can't believe you just asked me that! Like I would *miss* your baby shower. I am going to be an auntie! Well, not by blood, but by love."

"Yes, you are."

"I'll be there in an hour or so."

"That's perfect. Can you pick up Tabby? She would have called, but I told her I would take care of it. Bobbie is not going to get to the shower for a couple of hours, and Tabby's car in is the shop. Can you hook a sista up with a ride? Well, a sista's sista!"

"Uh--- I---"

"You uh what?"

"I can do that."

"Good, you know where she lives. She is already to go so anytime you get there is

©2012 Ghostwriter | Terry Birchwood

good. See you two later. Well, if you two don't—"

"You'll see us."

Oh shit. I have not been in a car with Tabby in years. And we are going to be alone! I will just be cool. There's nothing to it. Be cool, avoid eye contact, and keep my voice steady. There's nothing to it.

I was basically ready to get on the road. I touched myself up a little more – added a couple of accessories, and sprayed on my favorite scent.

I locked up and headed to Tabby and Bobbie's place. I knew the route well, make a left here, two miles down, right turn there, past the bank, and so on. You see, Tabby and Bobbie lived very close to one of the food places that Tabby and I used to go to on a regular basis.

We would get our favorite booth, if it were empty. When we first started dating, we would meet at Tanya's for dinner. The place has great food. My favorite is the salmon cakes, garden salad, brown rice, and lemon iced tea.

I remember Tabby filling up a straw with tea and shooting it on me. I returned the favor and we got sticky. The waiter was not happy with our liquid fight, but we tipped him enough for him to wipe the snarl off his face by the time we were leaving.

I have not been to Tanya's since I broke up with Tabby. I avoided certain memory triggers, and Tanya's place is one of them. Like I freaking needed *another* reason to think about her.

I remember once when we picked up take-out food. It was the first time at Tanya's. It was pouring outside and we got soaked, making that food trip, deciding Tanya's food was worth it. We hid the bags in our rainwear, but that didn't stop the rain from breaking through the paper bags.

We ran and laughed as we tried to run under trees and store canopies. We lost the race to remain dry. As soon as we got home, Tabby pushed me on the door, as I was closing it. She began to rub her wet face on mine, as she planted kisses on me.

She pushed my raincoat to the floor and she slowly kneeled on top of it. She then began to slowly undress and she tossed her clothes around the room. I leaned on the door and watched this wonderful display of seduction. I was so into Tabby.

She is so beautiful and to watch her slowly reveal her flesh to me was pleasurable. Her curves pulled me in. I walked toward her, and I grabbed her left breast and begin to play with it. My tongue found the hard nipple and began to make circles on it, bouncing it against my lips, and taking it into my mouth and then slowly, releasing it.

I held the other breast in my palm and I rotated my hand from side to side. I softly pinched at the nipple and made circles around it. I moved my hand all around the surface while I moved my tongue and lips from breast to breast.

Okay, now. Stop this right now. You CANNOT think about Tabby! You are almost at her place. You cannot let her read those thoughts in your damned head. Get it the fuck together! Come on Star! DON'T FUCK THIS UP! PULL IT TOGETHER! BE COOL!

Okay, I'm cool. Okay, turn left and bam. I took a deep breath, and called Tabby.

"Hey, Tabby."

"Hi Star."

"I'm outside when you're ready."

"Star, thanks so much for doing this."

"It's cool. Take your time. It's all good."

THIRTY - TABBY

I cannot believe Sam really called Star! I mean it makes sense, proximity-wise, but she knows I haven't been alone with Star for years, outside of a quick public run-in.

Okay, I really need to get outside and stop looking in the mirror. This is not a date. I don't see the problem with her picking me up, anyway. We are not lovers, 'friends with benefits', or anything remotely close. Chill out, Tab! Get a grip!

I saw her car parked in front of the house. I waved and walked toward her. I did not feel like I had a natural walk, as I was focusing on looking my best, strutting my best gait, getting her to stir. I wanted her to see what she was missing. I am still a little bitter, yes, wanting her to continue to pay for having that affair with that anonymous cowardly other lady fucking Star, bitch! *Okay, chill Tabby that was years ago.*

Star was standing in front of the car. "Hey Star. Again, thanks for this."

"You are welcome. Tabby. How are things? How is Bobbie?"

"I am good, Bobbie is good."

We got in the car, buckled our seatbelts and took off. I wanted to reach over and kiss her ear. But that was not happening.

We continued surface chatter about jobs, family, mutual friends, and current events. I just had to get through a half an hour in the car with Star. This was easy. I asked about Terry; she asked about Charles, and it went on and on for about ten minutes, and then there was silence.

The silence was excellent because I was in the sole company of Star. I could smell her sweet scent, I felt the heat from her body, and I wanted her all over me. *Ssh Ssh! Cool those thoughts!*

"Hey Tabby. Something is messing with me inside of my shoe. Do you mind if I pull over and take care of it. Whatever the hell it is, it is annoying."

"Star, do what you gotta do." I smiled.

"Cool. I may as well pull over in this Mall. That work for you?"

"Do you Star."

"Do I what?" Star looked at me in an intense way, with innocent curiosity across her face."

"Never mind, Star." I looked at her and smiled. "So, let's get to that foot. I'll stretch my legs while you take care of that, that thing." I smiled and pointed at her foot.

"That thing is much of nothing but enough to be annoying. That's for sure. I'll just be a minute, Tab."

The weather was perfect, not hot and not cold. It was a flawless breeze. I leaned on the passenger side of the car. Star always kept it so clean, inside and outside. I looked around at the shoppers on the grounds.

"How's that toe problem going?"

"Hey, I never said I have a toe problem. I said something's inside my shoe."

"Well did you get to that toe something, yet?" Star was sitting in the back seat. I walked around to see what was going on. She was shaking her shoe, searching for that something.

"Oh yea, gotcha, buddy. It's time to say goodbye sucker."

"Bravo. Now the foot is free of pain."

"For real. You know the smallest things sometimes annoy us the most."

"True, true."

"Hey, you wanna help an old body out of this back seat?"

"Sure."

I reached out my hand to help Star out of the back seat. Our bodies touched as she stood. The touch was that of a gentle brush, much like the breeze that played in the air. Oh my, I was on fire! It is unbelievable I could be consumed by pleasure from a swift touch. Before I realized what happened, I had let out a soft moan, the 'melody' as Star called it.

This is not supposed to happen. I am not supposed to feel these things. Star cheated on me! I must never let her think what she did is okay. Should I ever succumb to her deliciousness, I would be losing the battle of teaching her never to cheat on me. And, anyway, once a cheater, always a cheater!

I saw Star's lips part slightly as her eyes lowered a bit. For a brief moment, I forgot everything around us. We looked into each other's eyes and tears began to fill mine. I held them back, as I thought of that letter from Star's mistress. I cannot let Star into my life again! And, I am married!

Star looked at me with such concern. She seemed to love me so much, as if she was ready to do anything to push my tears back. How could she look at me this way? How can she love me this way and take a mistress during our relationship, and hide it? I really need to stop this now.

"Mmm, the breeze is beautiful. Can you smell the fresh air?" I wondered if that would work to change my thoughts.

"Yes, I smell the beauty of surroundings." Star closed her eyes and inhaled, deeply. She had the most peaceful smile on her face. She threw her head up to the sky and she stretched out her arms. Star is so beautiful. I miss you so much, Star. It is nearly unbearable.

I could not help but let my mind's thoughts fall into the rainbow she was spreading. "Well, we had better get going. You know Sam will take a bat to us for being late."

©2012 Ghostwriter | Terry Birchwood

THIRTY-ONE - SAM

"Hey Sam."

"Hi, Bobbie, glad you got here before the real fun started."

"Of course, you know I would not miss this, a restaurant business can't stop me from getting to you and my niece."

"You hope it's a girl. We'll find out soon enough. Soon enough."

"True, soon enough. Where's Chad the Dad? I've got something for him."

"Over there." I pointed.

"Ok, sweetie, I will say hello to daddy-to-be and see you in a minute."

"Ok." I smiled at Bobbie, and gave her a hug. She was nice, but something was always off between Bobbie and my sister. I could never put my finger on it.

Bobbie is gentle, loving, loyal, financially free, and she has other good qualities. She has never done anything that gave me a reason to dislike her. I don't dislike her. I just don't feel like I love her. I loved, well love, Star. She's like family. I don't know. Star and Tabby got something whether they want to face it or not.

My little boo signaled for my attention. "Hey baby. I feel you in there. How about you go easy on mommy." Tab passed by me as I talked with my little one.

"Hey, Tab, Bobbie's here. Did you see her?"

"Yes, I saw her, thanks."

"I never see you sparkle when I mention Bobbie, but you do when I mention Star. Why is that?"

"Don't you dare start with me Sam!"

"Okay, I'm sorry. Tab, I just want you happy again."

"I am happy."

"Oh really."

"Yes, really. What's with you? What is all this? Are you having cold feet about getting married or something and projecting that crap on me? I'll bet that's it. I should have figured this out earlier."

"Not a chance, Tab. This is really *all* about you. I want to see you shine again. Okay. Enough said. You know I love you Tab."

"I know Sam. I love you too. You still get on my nerves though, like right now!" Tabby gave me a quick hug, and she was off to mingle again.

The party was going great. I love my family and friends. I am one of the lucky ones, surrounded with people who love me, too. I am going to be a mom and also a wife, unbelievable stuff was going on with me.

THIRTY-TWO - STAR

"Hi sweets. You didn't have that bandage on a few minutes ago? What happened?"

"A dreadful paper cut from a damned paper plate! Can you believe this crap? By the way, do you want to help me heal? Lick my wounds, Star."

"I am going to pretend you did not just say that. You are a mess."

"For whose benefit, will you pretend that I didn't say it?"

"Whose benefit, what?"

"Never mind. You enjoying the shower?"

"Yeah, I love Sammie. She looks so happy."

"I agree. I wonder if I will have that with some one, some day."

"Uh, oh – you looking to get married and pop out some babies. You go Lexis. Is there something I should know?" I smiled to hint that I was kidding.

"I am not looking for it. But if it happens, I won't run away from it."

"I hear you. I can't even think about that."

"So, you've never thought about having a family, Star?"

"I didn't say that."

"Well, ok. Let's get in there and see those precious toys and things people bring to showers when they don't know when the baby is a boy or girl."

As Lexis got settled for the gift part of the party, I decided to get in a bathroom visit. As I reached for the door, it opened and there stood Tabby.

"Hey, you again?" Tabby smiled at me.

"Yeah, I'm afraid so."

"Why are you afraid?"

"Aah, you got jokes. Hmmm. What do you call a lesbian with big hands?"

"We are not going there, Star. You are still a hot mess."

"Why would I change? I am as I am."

"Ok, you getting all serious on me, now."

I smiled to lighten the tension in the air. I felt as if I was fighting not to take Tabby next to my body. I wanted, so badly, to pull her into me and taste her voluptuous lips.

"So, now it's my turn. Is there anything I should know about that bathroom?"

"Funny you mentioned that, Star. The toilet needs a little extra push when flushing. I think you'll figure it out. You've been here enough in the past. After all, well, anyway, you'll get it."

"I hope I get it."

Tabby motioned to move past me. I moved slightly to the left of the door and touched her hand as she passed. It was too late to pull back. My hand was rubbing the back of her hand. Tabby did not move her hand.

Instead, she took a deep breath and stood with me for a moment.

Realizing this could not happen, here, I let go of her hand. She turned to me with a face filled with confusion, stared into my eyes briefly, and then quietly walked toward the gathering crowd.

I waited a moment to allow time for Tabby to get back to Bobbie. Bobbie spent a lot of time looking at Tabby, so maybe Bobbie would not see me re-enter the area. Bobbie was not a stupid woman. I could not show my emotion and set her off on the prowl.

I promised not to upset Tabby's life with Bobbie, anyway. Bobbie seemed like a decent person. We were cool and I never heard word of Bobbie hurting Tabby. We are not friends, but we are cool.

I imagined life had I not let go of Tabby's hand a couple of minutes ago. Would we be standing in that spot slowly kissing each other, savoring every move of our tongues and lips, as we tasted each other?

Would we have shut the bathroom door and taken each other on the walls? Would I have put my hand in her panties and felt her silky den of delight?

Okay, enough of the 'what if' crap. Let's get back to the party. Chin up, head empty of last few minutes. *They never existed. They never existed. They never existed.*

As I positioned myself next to Terry, he whispered to me, "No you didn't."

"No, I didn't, what?"

"Girl, we will talk."

What is Terry talking about? I know he can't be talking about Tabby and me at the bathroom door. There was no one there but us. Well, that's all I saw. Uh oh, was I so caught up in that brief moment, that I missed the crowd watching Tabby and me? Oh shit!

Did Terry see us? Nah, I am bats. Terry is talking about something else. He has to be. No way did he see anything. Heck, we didn't do anything. So what, we were near the same bathroom. Okay, pull it together.

Everyone had formed a circle, of sorts, around the couch on which Sam sat. Chad stood near his wife-to-be. The 'ohs', 'ahs', and laughter took over the room and all was good, for now.

THIRTY-THREE - TABBY

It had been a couple of weeks since the shower and Star had finally made contact. I was relieved for the quick apology and glad she sent a text instead of calling. 'Sorry about the party, Star", that was enough without getting deep.

On the other hand, I wanted Star to knock down the front, walk up to me, kiss me, and have her way with me. Yes, I am a hot mess, in need of some meditation and prayer to wash my thoughts of adulterous hallways and rooms.

I could not understand how I could feel this way about someone that I no longer trusted. I didn't know how to shake these feelings. I tried everything – anger, denial, resistance, preoccupation, prayer, therapy – nothing worked.

I sang to myself when I thought of her. I counted sheep. I did everything. I even grabbed Bobbie, on occasion, and we made love. But, sadly, it was not much help. Again, it's not that I don't love Bobbie. But, that Star – she has a hook in me that I cannot seem to break free.

My mind tells me Bobbie has the qualities I want in a mate. My heart tells me Star has the qualities I want in a lover. No chance of having them both. I need to erase these foolish thoughts.

Which me should I listen to? The 'me' that whispers to my mind or the 'me' that whispers to my soul?

Ok, just because I am home alone does not mean I need to exhibit homely behavior. Refocus. Focus on SSS. Charles and I are about to make a lot of money. Oh, I need to call Charles. I also need to set up the monthly meeting with OFE. Oh, and make sure the remote workers all get the app upgrade. And, Sheila, yes, I need to order some more company shirts from her. And---

My to-do list prep was interrupted by a ring tone. It was Bobbie's phone I heard ringing. I cannot believe she forgot it. She never forgets her phone. Maybe it's her calling the phone to find it. She'll probably laugh when I answer it.

I walked over to the phone and took a peek. Well, it's not her. Who is Richie? Ok, don't be nosey. She will get the message later.

I picked up Bobbie's phone and began to walk it over to the kitchen counter so she would see it as soon as she came in. It rang again. And it was Richie. Ok, ignore it. It is not your phone.

I placed the phone on the kitchen counter, as Bobbie always stopped here to check the mail when she got home. She would see it as soon as she walked in the door.

Oh goodness, the phone rang again! Richie again. Ok, this must be important.

I picked up the phone and before I could say anything, I heard, "Hey sweet pussy. I can't wait to get some. It's been a week. You miss big dick daddy? I'll bet Tabby doesn't give it to you like I do. See you at six. Keep it moist for me, baby."

The phone fell from my hand and the room began to whirl. I started to uncontrollably shake and tears streamed down my face.

Please tell me I was hearing things. Please tell me that was the wrong number. Please tell me that male voice did not just call my name. Please tell me the 'Richie' I heard on the phone did not sound like the Richard Watson whom was now an SSS partner. Please tell me I was dreaming or inhaled some medical incredible. This is not real. This is not real. This is not real.

By the time I picked up the phone, Richie was no longer on the line. What the *fuck* is going on?

THIRTY-FOUR - STAR

I miss Tabby in ways she could never imagine. She was my heart, soul, and mind's playmate. God, what did I do to deserve this? That relationship felt so *right*! What went wrong? I know I could have fought harder to keep her, but she was so, so mad. I never saw Tabby like I saw her the night she told me to get out, and basically, don't look back.

How could I beg Tabby? She was not going to change her mind, and I was so blinded to what was happening that I had no ground to stand on to make a case, let alone fight a battle. That same morning, before she blew her lid, we had made love.

"Star, oh! That's it baby. Right there. Oh, baby. That is so good. Mmm!"

I was so into Tabby's body, I barely knew of my surroundings. My head was nestled in her cleavage, as she held on to my face with her hands. I felt her breath rise and fall as I fingered her pussy. I played in the soft hairs that protected the garden, getting them comfortable so they would fall back to unveil the pleasures.

Tabby continued breathing deeply as her hands moved all over my body, wherever she could reach. She knew how much I loved to feel her hands on my skin. Her hands were like the bow to my fiddle; her every touch electrified me. No one had ever brought these feelings out of me before. I wanted to give her all of me. And I wanted to take all of her.

As I kept stroking Tabby's clitoris, I began to lick one of her nipples. She was sitting up on the bed, rocking back and forth, slowly, her body letting me know it was enjoying the attention. I could feel her lips pulsating, about to take me inside of her whether I was ready or not.

I still had on my pants and I had a special treat for Tabby this morning. Seven was here for a visit. Tabby would slowly move her eyes from whatever she was touching on my flesh to the strong rod that lay beneath my silk fabric. As her hand would brush the big tickler, she would also graze my leg, sending shivers through me.

I began to take Tabby in my mouth, as I continued to nestle her playground. She hungrily kissed at my lips, licking them quickly and then slowly. I pulled away from her lips. She kissed the top of my shoulder and removed my top. She grabbed my breast and held on to it as I slid two fingers inside her. "Ooh, ooh, ooh!"

The window was cracked and a perfect wind crept through the room. Our bodies became moist enough to glow, but the wind kept us from working up dripping sweats. Tabby pushed down on my fingers and clenched her vagina. I held still.

Tabby leaned into my chest and held onto my back. I kissed the side of her face, her neck and shoulders. I placed my other hand on her ass and pulled her closer to me. I pulled my fingers halfway out of her pleasure and held them still for a moment. Tabby's lips quivered, uncontrollably.

I slowly pushed my fingers back in her and moved them around. As I grazed her walls she sighed and twitched. I, again, put my tongue in her mouth slowly. I softly bit her top lip. "Oh, fuck me", Tabby whispered.

I pulled my hand completely out of Tabby and I licked my pinky. She tasted sweet.

I stood up and began to remove my pants. Tabby looked at Seven and then she took off her top. Her body was so beautiful, to me. I could never get enough of physical play with Tabby. I felt alive, adventurous, and curious.

"Mr. Officer. Is that your club or are you just happy to see me?" Tabby looked at me with seduction, innocence, and curiosity, all at once.

"Ma'am, I am really happy to see you and this is my club, Seven is the name."

"Well, Seven, nice to meet you." Tabby grabbed Seven in a handshake and pulled in her direction. Tabby kneeled on the edge of the bed, facing the wall. She then pushed her hair away and looked at me. She parted her lips just enough for me to see the tip of her tongue. She then threw her head back, and licked her lips.

I stood behind her and placed the tip of Seven right outside of her vagina. I placed it perfectly to the frame of her entry. Tabby was so wet and her body was jumping to my touch. I rubbed my hands around her ass and grabbed her cheeks. I bumped the outside of her pussy just enough for friction, but not enough to enter her. There was no rush. She is so delicious. Why rush a delicious meal? Savor it.

"Damn, Tabby. Hmmm. You feel so fucking incredible. Hmmm."

"You feel me? Can you feel this?" With that question, Tabby reached behind her and put her hand on my ass, pulling me deeper inside of her. I tunneled down a couple of inches and stopped. Tabby was still holding on to my ass, clenching and slowly raking her nails on me.

Tabby moved forward on the bed, and I followed until I found myself on my knees behind her. Tabby stayed on her knees and secured her hands on the headboard. I moved into her until I was again hovering outside of her sweet doors. I took my hand

and began to caress her breast, making circular motions around her nipple, as it stood at attention.

My other hand guided Seven back inside of Tabby. As soon as I got in, I stopped. She ached and let out a moan. "Aah, shit! Mmm, Mmm, Mmm. Yes, Star, take it."

I placed my hand on her backside for some leverage and then I began to milk Tabby's walls with delight. I rocked Seven back and forth inside of her. Each time I went deeper and made wider motions, expanding the spaces I was tickling inside of her. Tab was clenching the headboard with both hands and slowly grinding on Seven. She pushed back and forth. Tabby wanted to give her pussy to me, and I wanted to take it.

I felt Tabby's vagina creating such a slick pathway for me to twist and turn to tap all of her hidden pleasure spots. Tabby moved her hands from clenching the headboard to holding on to the wall. She had her head held back and her hair brushed me as I plunged in and out of her.

We were breathing heavily, moaning and shaking as we went to a higher and higher level of passion. "Fuck me Star!" I held on to Tabby's hip with one hand and fondled the moist button between her legs.

Whoa? Who is interrupting my memory-lane sex with Tabby? Amazing, it was the woman of my dream, Tabby. Tabby never calls so I answered the phone with a little trepidation.

"Star, I need to see you right away. Meet me at Tanya's, *please*."

THIRTY-FIVE - STAR

"Hey, Tabby. What's going on?"

"I have a big problem. I want to wait until Sam gets here to talk about it."

"Whoa, it's that big huh. What is it? Never mind, I can wait. Tab, you don't look good. Are you sure you want to wait. I haven't seen you like this since…wait…you and Bobbie having problems?"

"Why do y'all do this to me?"

"Do what Tabby?"

"Cheat on me?"

"I never cheated on---"

"I give you a faithful hand in partnership. I am attractive, smart, loving, and you give me lies, in return."

"Wait, Tab, catch me up here."

"I'm sorry. Sam should be here any minute, and I won't have to catch her up. I'm sorry

I called you, Star. I shouldn't get you involved in this."

"Tab, your business is my business, when you want it to be. I love you."

"Star, how can you love me? That note told me different."

"What note?"

"You know what note."

"Remember, Tab she doesn't know about the note." I heard Sam breaking into the conversation, from behind me.

"What note, Sam?"

"I would love to tell you, Star, but it's not my place. I gave Tab my word."

"Hey guys, I am right here!" Tabby said.

"Hey babe, tell me what's going on that you needed to call me out of a date with food at Yugliani's buffet. This had better be so important, girl."

"Bobbie is cheating on me."

"What!" exclaimed Sam. "I didn't hear you correctly? Okay. What did you just say?"

"You heard me, Bobbie is cheating on me."

I was stunned and sat in silence. I heard Tabby say, "Earth to Star. You hear me?"

"Oh yes, I heard you. I am just shocked. Are you sure about this?"

"Oh, I am sure."

"Are you, Star?"

"What's that supposed to mean, Sam?"

"You know what it means. You have no proof that Star---"

"That Star what?" I asked. What on earth were they talking about?

"This is not the time. No offense, Star, but you and I are history. I called you both here because I have a big problem, now. I need some guidance."

"Okay, spill it. Tell us."

"Well, Bobbie forgot her cell phone this morning. It rang several times from the same person. I finally answered but before I said anything, a male voice began to talk about seeing Bobbie tonight to give her some dick."

"What? Oh no. How do you know it wasn't the wrong number?"

"Because he said' I bet Tabby doesn't give it to you like I do' or something like that!"

"Oh Shit."

"Now, do you think I'm sure?"

"Tabby, I am so sorry. I knew there was something about Bobbie that wasn't right. She always seemed nice, but not right. That bi---, I mean bozo! I cannot believe it, well, maybe I can. Like I said, something just wasn't right about her."

"Oh my God, Tab. I am so sorry for this. I cannot imagine what you are feeling."

"You should be able to imagine."

"What does that mean?"

"Tell her, Tab."

Sam continued to egg on Tabby. "May as well get it all on the table. You are asking her to guide you with your problem. So, guide her with her problem. Help her to understand why you left her."

"Look Sam, this is---"

"Look Tabby, enough already. If you don't tell her, I will. I swear! You've held this theory; I repeat theory, not even fact, for all these years. Let it go. Let Star know so she can find peace. *Dammit*, Tab, do it because it's the *right thing* to do!"

"You wouldn't, Sammie."

"Oh, yes I will. Don't try me today, Tab. You have no right to leave on theory, I told you this, years ago. I am sick of watching you two---"

"You two what? We have moved on."

"Tell her Tab. Now, Tabitha."

"Okay. I will make this brief and we can get back to why I need you now. Deal?"

"Deal, anything is better than nothing." Sam retorted.

"Okay, here it goes. Star, the reason I broke up with you is because I found out you were cheating on me. One of your playmates sent me a note. She claimed you and her belonged together. She mentioned things, in that note, which I thought only you and I shared. She was obviously on some type of *inside* with you or should I say, you were *inside* of her!"

"Tab, are you serious? I don't know what you're talking about. I did not have a mistress. I have never had a mistress."

"Sure Star, put another wound in me, right now, and deny it after I have proof. I got the fucking note, Star!"

"That's no proof. What proof? What's in this note that only you and I should know?"

"Too fucking much! Sorry, Sam. She knew that I snore, and she saw my fingers tattooed on your ass. Oh, she knew about that corny fucking line you used when talking about sex for the first time, *'I don't bring women into my bedroom unless I want to mate with them.'* Yeah, that fucking line! Sorry Sam."

Sam was singing to the baby to override our curses. I was listening to Tab's outpouring, more like revelation for me.

"I can't believe you were fucking cheating. She said you loved her more than me. When I thought about it, I thought 'Maybe she's right. You loved her enough to tell her the truth about me. But you did not love me enough to tell me the truth about her."

"Tabby, I do not know what you are talking about. This is not true!"

"Star you hurt me so badly. You ran me into the arms of what I felt I lost with you – security. That's what I thought Bobbie was for me. Haha, at least I thought she was. Boy, was I fucking wrong! Sorry Sam."

I was sitting, staring into Tabby's eyes, simply taken aback. These words were so foreign to me. I had no fucking idea what she was talking about! AND THIS IS WHY SHE LEFT ME!!! So, it turns out, I lost the love of my life over a lie.

Tabby went on about how I betrayed her and how she fell for my bullshit. She talked about the things we shared together and how I had betrayed her, how everything must have been a lie, how once a pimp, always a pimp. And, she went on and on.

A headache set in as I listened to Tabby. "Tabby, why didn't you tell me this five years ago? I can't believe this. I lost you over a lie!"

"I told you it might not be true, Tabby."

"Ok, now Sammie, I am supposed to just say, "Oh I believe you Star, I made a mistake, let's make-up!"

180 Ghostwriter; Terry Birchwood

"Well, that would be a good start, especially since Bobbie ---"

"Bobbie fucking did the same thing!"

"It's not the same thing. I never slept with another woman from the first day I met you, Tab. You should be giving me the benefit of the doubt. You should have talked with me and given me the benefit years ago? Who is this lying bitch anyway? What's her name?"

"She didn't tell me her name."

"No name, a note, no proof and you dump me. I cannot believe what I am hearing. Pinch me Sam."

"Tab, I told you. Look at her. She has no clue what you are talking about. You know she doesn't!"

"How do I know?"

"Tab, I love you just as much as I always have, and that is a lot. I had no need to hold an affair on the side. You knew how satisfying you were for me. You were my

Ms. Delicious. You saw what we did. You were there! We had such a magnificent love affair. I loved you Tab, and I still do."

Tabby looked at me, but I was not sure if she was really listening. Taking the chance she might be, I kept talking.

"I think about you all of the time. I never think about you with regrets, because I have none. I am innocent of this lie put before you. I love you and savor everything we had together. I still smell you, feel you, see you, sense you, touch you, and make love to you. I know it's all in my mind, but it is my world. You are my world. Still."

"Star, I can't do this right now. I know it might sound selfish, but I need both of you to help me with this Bobbie thing. Star, you have my word we can talk about this later. I promise. Okay?

"Ok."

"Okay so, I forgot to tell you, the caller's name is Richie and it sounds like Richard Watson from OFE."

"What the---? This cannot get any messier."

"Yes it can because I am going to set this off. If I am lucky, Richie won't bring up the call when he sees Bobbie. There was nothing discussed that she would need to remember when she sees this Richie."

"I still can't believe Bobbie is tipping out, and with a man!" Sam piped in.

Tab continued on. "Oh yes, Bobbie is definitely cheating. And if this guy really is Richard Watson, this goes deeper than cheating. Something must be up with the partnership, if it's him. If Bobbie would do this, I imagine she will do anything. I need to get my assets and SSS some protection, set Richie and Bobbie up for a fall, and then deal with the note and you, Star. Is that fair enough for you?"

"Tab, I will give you what you ask me to give to you. Let me know what to do."

"And you know I've got your back, pregnant or not. What's going on my to-do list?"

"I love you both. I mean, you two are my favorite people, always there for me. It means a lot to me. Blood or no blood, you have always made me feel like you truly have my back even after all I have been through with the both of you. Okay, enough of that mush, let's plan the royal fuck of Bobbie and Richie. Sorry, Sam. I will get used to this curse-free zone, soon."

"Probably be too late then. The baby will be here." We all laughed.

"To the royal couple."

"Yes, to the royal couple."

We clicked our beverage glasses together. A little orange juice spilled on Tabby's fingers. I wanted to lick them.

Hmm. Tabby was going to be a free agent again. And, we broke up over a lie! We talked and talked about how to best secure all of her assets linked to Richie and Bobbie, and pull this off undetected.

Tabby's lover and Tabby's new business partner are fucking each other? This is unfucking believable. What a planet.

Before we realized it, a couple hours had passed. Long hugs, quick kisses, and teary eyes sent us on our way."

"Tabby, you know you can call me any time. Any time, Tabby I mean it. I think we've got a good plan put together, and you will be okay. I know it sounds cliché, but you will get over this. Heck, you got over me."

Tabby was actually meeting Richard for lunch; what a bitch. Sam and Chad had an appointment with her obstetrician. I needed to head to the office to catch up with Lexis about some California office paperwork.

While driving, I thought about love and how it creates such passion roller coasters. I thought about movies where love appeared to defy everything, such as my love for Tabby. I thought of the greats, usually famed through breaking barriers of class, gender, race, religion, politics, and culture. Most of our great classic movies standing on love, peace, and war are based around a love story involving a couple that society thinks should not unite – Romeo and Juliet, West Side Story, and Beauty and The Beast.

Why are we so hung up on whether some one has a penis or vagina between his or her legs? Why does it matter if someone's skin is dark or light? Who cares if your grandmother was from a different country than your grandfather? Why should it matter to me who you love? Who am I to determine love's rules? Who is anybody to do that? To me, this all a stupid waste of time, trying to control love. Silly.

Instead of trying to instill our forefathers and our own nonsensical control on each other, let's just try to practice good deeds. It's the only rule we truly need. Follow that, and we are all good, across the globe. We need to just love each other without any boundaries.

Another driver's horn blasting and cursing brought me back to the moment. I was almost at MyBody.

THIRTY-SIX - RICHARD

"Damn, Richie. I hate waiting so long for this."

"Me too baby." I took Bobbie like she was a rag doll. Just knowing she was sleeping with a woman fired me up to show her who Daddy is in this place. I held Bobbie in the air, just above my waist, as I pinned her back on the wall. I pushed her up and down on my shaft, fucking her deeper with each push. She held on to my neck.

"That' it Richie. Fuck me! Fuck me! Fuck me! Shit Richie, Fuck me! Faster, baby, Ooh yeah, that's it Richie, fuck me good."

I couldn't hold out. That pussy all around my dick called on my load to shoot into the condom. Bobbie was clinging to me and pushing so hard, I almost fell backward. She sure could fuck deep, and hard, just the way I like it.

I imagined being with her and Tabby. I could see them making love on the bed. I would come over unexpected and find myself to their bedroom, with an innocent look. Yea, I know Tabby is a lez, but I could see myself fucking her. She is fine. I would make her forget all about sucking pussy. I would finger fuck her ass with these big hands and make her forget all about dykes.

"What in the fuck are you thinking about Richie?"

"What the hell you talking about?"

"I saw you. I see that look. Where the hell are you?"

"Damn, Bobbie. Don't fuck up the mood."

"You already did that Richie. I know when you are not into me."

"I am in you. What are you talking about? I just came. Can't a guy get a minute to reset his nuts get back to normal? You know how you pull at my balls and that shit wears me out. You take my dick on rides, baby."

Bobbie calmed down. "Just checking, Richie. I need to make sure you're not going to do to me with someone else what we are doing to Tabby."

"Are you kidding me? You know how I feel about you. Don't put me through this shit right now. I gotta go, anyway and deal with your bitch."

"She's not my bitch. She is *a* bitch! You don't fuck with Bobbie!"

"I like fucking with, Bobbie. I want to fuck her again, now, but I gotta go."

Bobbie was putting her pants back on, and I washed up in the kitchen. If only her staff knew what we did in this restaurant, they could never look at it the same way again.

Bobbie has the biggest balls I had ever seen on a woman. When I first met her, she was seductive, fly, and spicy at the mouth. She had a way of saying things that made you think she was a bitch, but she was so fucking fine, it did not matter what she said. I just wanted to fuck her.

We met before she got hooked up with Tabby. I was at a party and there she was, across the floor looking unapproachable, but so fine I had to dare myself to get under her skin, well in her pants.

We soon began fucking around, on and off, for years. She knew I was married, and she was not interested in being tied down, so it worked. I have never fooled around on my wife with a woman for this long. I think I love her, but she is such a cunning bitch that I can never fully trust her. But it's good. We fuck each other good, scheme great together – she is my hood lady.

I know she has my back. She's proven it over the years, been there when my dad got on my nerves, was there when mom died, and she even liked me before I got a position at the company, when I was still trying to find myself. What are you going to do with that? Can't let it go – fine, loyal, cunning bitch – what a package. Cake at home and ice cream with Bobbie.

I remembered when she first told me about this deal that would generate endless income. I was naturally intrigued. Bobbie always had grand plans to set shit off.

It wasn't until I got interested in getting in on the deal that I learned of personal ties between Bobbie and the deal victims. She would get so indignant about Tabby that I finally asked her what was the beef between the two of them.

She told me she was an undercover lesbian. She blew me away with the details of being married to her enemy. I had no idea Bobbie was leading this double life, especially since I was living mine in the open. She knew I was married. I wondered why she didn't tell me she was married.

In the past she had always maintained that we should never go to her place or my place for a rendezvous because anybody could be watching and link us to our personal lives. It never occurred to me it was because she had a person in her life.

I thought I would be angry, but interesting enough, that shit turned me on. I saw me fucking them both.

"I'll call you."

"Cool. Touch it once before you go."

Bobbie pushed her pussy at me. I pushed toward her. Uh oh, time to go. If my dick rises again, I'll be late for sure. Baby! Bobbie sure can fuck.

THIRTY-SEVEN - BOBBIE

On my way home from Café Gallery, I drifted to the tasks ahead of me. I had come so far with my plan of action. I could not believe I waited all these years to get even with this bitch. Years and years were gone. But it was soon to pay off.

Even though life was better now, I remembered life wasn't so good back then, when that bitch nearly ruined my life forever. I had second and third degree burns. My leg was broken in two places, three cracked ribs, two broken fingers, and cuts and bruises from head to toe.

That bitch almost killed me on the road after that frat party. You would think she could put two and two together after reading the story in the paper. I think she knows what she did and she just didn't give a damn. I hate her.

I imagine she might have been too wasted to notice. I imagine she did not notice, in her rear view mirror, that I had suddenly swerved and went off the small bridge. I guess she did not hear the crash as my car rolled down the steep hill, or the sound of the explosion as fire filled the air and car, or my cries for help.

But I saw her, that night. I saw her license plate as I was suddenly approaching her car, not realizing she was in front of me that night. That license emblazoned in my memory, TAB BEE, unforgettable. If that bitch had put her night-lights on, I would have seen her, sooner than before being up her ass, on that clear, open road.

Yes, TAB BEE. I already knew the license plate name from around campus. And, I already knew of Tabby. She hung out with Charles. Charles and I knew each other. I thought he was genius and I wanted to work with him some day. I knew he would do well in life, and I wanted to be a part of it. I loved developing software as much as he did. And I had a big secret crush on him.

Somewhere along the way of getting to know Charles, this Tabby girl and he bonded. She wasn't so cute back then, but Charles was more interested in her than me. I didn't like her from the gate.

It took me years to recover from the accident. I had been drastically damaged, emotionally, mentally, and physically. I had countless hospital stays and visits to correct bones, close wounds, and graft skin. I never graduated from undergrad school. I lost the scholarship to Harvard, my family drained their savings on my operations, and I was in pain for what seemed like ever.

Back when it happened, I couldn't even pick up a book to read, my eyes hurt when they were open because of the burns and scars all over the lids, brows and other portions of my face. Tabby knew I had scars and she knew I was in a car crash, long ago, but she did not know where the accident took place.

"Ma'am, ma'am. You're gonna have to turn here. The street, ahead, is closed."

"Okay, thanks Officer." Damn, I was almost home and now I need to detour. That's another ten minutes added on for sure.

I'd better call Tabby. I have to stick to the doting role, as much as it fucking drives me crazy. It will pay off, though.

"Hey, Tabby, I just got detoured and it looks like I'll be passing the ice cream shop. Can I get you something?"

"Ice cream sounds good, you pick. I'll see you when you get in. Be safe."

"Ok, see you soon, love ya."

"Love ya too."

Tabby is such a stupid one. I think I gave her too much credit in college. I cannot believe she thinks I love her. Can't she see the fire in my eyes, the masked hell bent agenda against her. She must not be able to feel, just as I thought back then. How can she not feel that I don't love her?

Well, I know one thing she's gonna feel. She will feel pain in a little over a year. She will feel pain.

Okay, enough of that. Gotta get in character for the rest of the evening. I love Tabby, I love Tabby, I love Tabby…

THIRTY-EIGHT - LEXIS

I did everything on my list. I got close to her, I sabotaged her relationship, I was there for her during the good, bad and ugly times, and I gained her trust.

Add to that, I look fantastic, I am smart, and I give her whatever she asks of me. So, why in the hell are we still not together years later?

I have told her I want her. I have shown that I want her. I have asked to date her. We have fun when we're together. We get each other.

Damn, Star? Why don't you want me as a lover? It's so easy for you to tell me that you cannot imagine life without me – as a business partner! The public loves us. We are a dynamic couple. Why doesn't she see this like I know it to be?

One day she will come around. I just have to be patient. Eventually she will see what is just in front of her nose and what's been missing in her bed, me.

"Hey, Lexis"

"Hey Star, what's up?"

"It's all good."

"Yeah, I know Star, it's all good here too. You need something?"

"I just want to catch up on the West Coast staffing. Any luck with the ads?"

"Actually, yes, I have eight or nine Skype interviews next week. The hiring pool is great, overall. I think we can pick three of them. I already know everything there is to know about them."

"I know you do. You are the best in the business, you know that."

I smiled at Star. When she smiled back, I turned away nonchalantly, but inside I was burning with desire. I couldn't let her see how in love with her I was, not yet. I wished she would walk up to me and say, "You know, Lexis, we need to talk. I see my nose now. I love you."

She would grab me like she used to grab Tabby. There wasn't a rumor on the street that did not involve great when it came to gossip about Star's sexual knack and abilities. I wanted some of that for a long time, and I still want it.

I realized I had to have Star when I first met her. We met at a ballet premiere. In the lobby after the performance, she walked toward me and then she asked if I had met any of the cast, yet. I thought her question innocent enough. I said, "No." She told me her cousin was one of the male dancers, the one with the neon orange tights in the opening ballet. I told her I thought he was a good dancer.

She looked at me as if I was the only person in the room. Well, that's what I thought at the time until a woman came beside her and laced her fingers with Star's fingers. But it was already too late. I was madly in love with this woman that seemed to know all of me in a glance.

Dammit, notice me already. "Okay, Lexis. I've got a meeting downtown with a solid prospect. You remember, Meadow Sinsberg.

She's interested in a group contract for 25 seniors to come in once per week. The more contracts the better."

"I'm with you there. Good luck. I'm sure you'll close the deal. Remember, you are the second best in the business."

"Aha, you funny. Second to none."

"Touché. Later, Star."

"Later."

And she was gone again. I know I went to some serious lengths to capture this woman, but that's life right. That note to Tabby, I thought that would do it. Star would be devastated and fall in my arms one night. That backfired. Instead, she shut down completely.

I remember thinking I had the perfect note. I took my time to include things that I overheard or saw. I saw the tattoo on Star, when she and Tabby left the office door cracked. One night, I came back to the office for something and there they were, all over each other in Star's office.

Star was standing over Tabby, with her beautiful bare ass exposed. I saw a tattoo of two fingers on Star's ass, well, that's what it looked like from where I was standing or should I say hiding. I had never seen fingers on an ass so I never forgot it. Of course, I never made myself known. I left as quietly as I entered.

I learned to keep my eyes and ears extremely alert around the office, in case I could catch some more private moments between the two of them.

It wasn't until weeks later that I learned the fingers on Star's ass were those of Tabby. One, afternoon, I had transferred a call to Star and somehow I turned on three-way conference.

It was very quiet in my office and the nosey in me got the best of me. They did the cooing shit for a minute, and then I heard Tabby ask Star, "How are my fingers treating you, baby? I love that my fingers are always tapping your ass, keeps you on your toes."

All that planning, and I still don't have Star. 'Fuck' be me. Well, at least I get to see her, spend time with her, and dine with her. So what if it is all on the pretenses of business. We do a lot of things that dating couples do, but I don't think she realizes it yet. We just don't fuck. She will figure it out one day. Time takes care of everything.

©2024 Ghostwriter | Terry Birchwood

THIRTY-NINE - TILLY

"Hey, Tilly! What's up? What are you doing around here?"

"Hey Chad. I'm meeting a friend for lunch across the street. How about you?"

"Well you know pregnancy cravings. Sam's cravings got me all over the place, finding her crazy foods."

I laughed at Chad's comment. He always seemed almost perfect, which is why I didn't trust him. Dumb me, trying to spy and already discovered!

"So, good seeing you Chad. Tell Sam, I'll call her in the morning."

"Ok, Tilly. Take care."

We exchanged brief hugs and Chad headed off on his errand. Even though I was not meeting anyone, I decided to go into the café and get a cup of tea.

While waiting, I thought about Sam. What if she gets so into motherhood that she doesn't return to work? What will I do? What if she offers to sell me the company? What if she sells her portion of the company to someone else? Okay, this is silly. Sam's going nowhere.

"Is that you, Tilly?" What? Who now?

I peeked around to meet Tabby in the face.

"Oh my gosh Tab, you will never believe, I just saw Chad. Is there a party y'all not telling me about?" We chuckled.

"If you don't know, I don't know either!"

"What are you having? Maybe that'll help me decide."

"Nothing special, Til. It's green tea with a Splenda, nothing complicated."

"Hmm. That sounds good. Anyway, what are you up to, Tab?"

"Just wanted some tea, and this is my favorite local place. You know how it is – we want what we want."

"I know that feeling."

"Have you talked to Sam today? I need to call her."

"Funny you mention that. I told Chad I am going to call her in the morning. I have been working on giving her days without office work. She needs time to enjoy the process of bringing a child into this world."

"You *know* I don't know from experience, but I have always felt birth is amazing and should not be taken for granted. To pop out of air, sperm and egg, just the thought is awesome to me."

"Telling it like it is, as always." We chuckled.

"I still can't believe Sam is pregnant. It's ironic that she never got pregnant with her other husbands. Maybe Chad is the one."

"And maybe, he is not the---. Never mind."

"Oh, back up! I am not going to miss the end of that sentence. Not the what?"

"It's probably nothing, Tabby."

"What's nothing?"

"Well, I just have a funny sense about Chad. He is almost perfect and that bothers me. Sam never talks about things that irritate her, nothing he does where she feels he needs a retraining, no ill word about his bad habits, nothing. Don't you think that is weird that she can find nothing to complain about? Don't you?"

"Well, several years ago, I would probably have agreed with you, but since…well since I was with someone where nothing ever felt imperfect, I have to say it is possible. And you know Sam, sweetie. She does nothing she does not want to do, and if she takes a dent later, as a result, she will get back up. You know the cliché, 'she's a big girl'."

"Yes, I hear you. I know that I am probably overreacting, but I just want her happy. And you know her luck, her first husband cheated on her with her best friend."

"And you are her best friend, now. And, I am fairly confident that will not happen.

Hell, you barely like Chad, from what I hear right now."

We laughed out loud.

"So it's your turn to back up. What is this with your comment about you 'were' with someone where nothing ever felt imperfect? *You were*?"

"That's not important. What is important is that Sam loves Chad. He makes her happier than I have seen her. I cannot take that away from her. If he turns out to be an asshole, let her, at least, enjoy now, being a mother-to-be, and a bride-to-be, of great family and friends. Can you do that? I know you can. Do it for Sammie."

"Of course, Tab. Thanks for this. If I turn out to be right, it will devastate her during a most vulnerable time. If I turn out to be wrong, I'll have wasted a lot of money on a detective!"

We laughed again.

FORTY - TABBY

It was in those moments talking with Tilly, that I *accepted* what I ran from these past years. I still love Star immensely. I tried to shake it off to lust, and this and that but, it all adds up to love.

I completely understood what my sister had been telling me all along. How could I have pushed Star away so easily? She seemed so honest when she denied having a mistress. But on the other hand, Bobbie seemed to love me so much, and look what that bitch is doing?

"Tilly, I love you for taking care of Sam, it means the world to me."

"Tab, I am not taking care of her by choice. We are just supposed to do it, I guess. You know I don't let many people close to me. Sam, though, she's different. I think you know what I mean."

"I gotcha. She is something else. Lord only knows." I smiled at Tilly and we chatted a while longer."

208 - Ghostwriter | Terry Birchwood

I had so much to do to make sure I stayed ahead of Bobbie. I was happy when she called to find out if I wanted something from the store. It gave me a chance to get my character in normal range before she got home.

I was still trying to mask my anger, so I had decided to get some quick air before she got home. So, I walked to the cafe, and cleared my head by running into Tilly.

Once Tilly and I finished up, it took me less than a minute to return home. I was already praying that I would not let on that I knew of Bobbie's adultery by throwing this piping hot tea in her fucking face. Be cool, Tabby, cool, breathe, in, out.

Before I knew it, Bobbie was home. "Hey babe. Look what I got for you."

I wanted to smash that ice cream in her face, but instead, I replied, "You are so sweet Bobbie. I don't know what I would do without you."

"It's nothing, babe. That's what I do for my boo. So, how was your day? Anything new?"

You have no idea how new. Instead, I said, "my day was good, the usual, meetings, plans, clients, blablabla. How about your day, honey?"

"You already know my boring day, cook, supervise, and run the office. Boring maybe, but I can bring home the bacon, fry it up and serve it to you. I want you to never worry about anything."

Yeah, worry about anything except you, trifle-butt. Bobbie was good at playing the game of an all-loving spouse. But from the call with Richie, it seemed she was actually was a dick-starved whore. Well, let's play Bobbie.

"So sweetie, are you feeling like a fisher tonight? Mamma wants to share her ice cream with you."

"It depends on what the fisher will be trying to catch."

Oh you are gonna catch something whether you want it or not. It's called Hell, you lying bitch whore.

Let's play bitch. I am going to shove pussy in your face every chance I get. You will be running out the door for that dick, and to avoid me locking your ass up for life. Let's play, Bobbie. Welcome to the Royal Fuck, and I am your hostess, Tabby.

FORTY-ONE - STAR

"What's up Stardust?"

"Hey Terry, we need to talk in person."

"Yeah, we do girl. I didn't forget about the shower. I told you that we need to talk, girl. Don't act like this is your idea."

"Whoever's idea it is, meet me at Guzman's in an hour."

"Will be there." And he hung up.

Terry had amazingly powerful connections in his network. I was confident he would be able to recommend resources to help Tabby protect herself from Bobbie as the scandal and divorce unfolded.

I was definitely sad for Tab going through this, never wanting to see her hurt, for anything. Fucking Bobbie up seemed quite appealing right now.

My mind was heavy on destroying Bobbie, but my heart and soul were focused on protecting Tabby, and using positive means to come to this end. There would be nothing good coming out of any physical violence from Tabby, or any of us that were uniting to stand by her.

I got myself ready to meet Terry. I checked my calendar, with Lexis, and on my emails.

"Hi Ghostwriter. Write.

Tabby"

I could not hide my smile when I got this email. Hmm. Write.

"I sense a surrender to your sweet allure. My breath tracks your breath. My eyes are stuck on roaming you. My lips are craving your taste. My tongue dances with yours and tastes your succulent lips…"

Nah. I am too excited, I need to calm down and write this later. I don't want Tabby to mix up with me right now. It's not good. She needs to deal with her situation. She is not leaving Bobbie for me; she is leaving Bobbie because of Bobbie. Don't be an ass, Star. Focus, focus.

Okay, time to go.

As I was pulling up to meet Terry, I saw him entering the restaurant. Terry had such a distinguished way about him. I recognized him from any direction.

"Hey babe. You are right on me. Did you follow me here? Tail me?"

"You are feeling yourself, obviously."

"Can you blame me? I am irresistible. And, you know it, Stardust."

We sat down, and Terry wasted no time running his mouth. I loved him. He was one to get to the point and move on.

"Look, Stardust, I know you have feelings for Tabby, and I know she has feelings for you, no matter what you say. I think you, two, need to have a conversation. Not to get back together or anything. Just, maybe finally talk it out after all these years. You both seem to hold on to something, that is clearly more than friendship, and maybe if you talk, you can let it go, whatever it is – love, hate, I don't know. And--"

"And, Terry. How was your day? It's good to see you? Can I get a hug first?"

"Honey, you know how I do? It's nothing personal. I just get it out so we can move on and enjoy the rest of the day. No need building up to it, beating around a damned bush. Spit it out and then let's just eat. You know me, Star, so don't start that 'And, Terry, how way your day' crap'."

"Oh, are we on the la period Madame?"

"How'd you know girl, is it really showing?"

"Never, you are flawless, Theresa."

"Ok, now you have lost your mind. That's Mr. Theresa. Don't forget. I know I am a man, and—"

"Oh no. Don't start. You know I know after all these years. And how dare you pull that shit with me. Do I get all defensive and obnoxious when your ass calls me StarDick? Huh, Terry?"

"Touché, okay, anyway about you and Tabby. What's up? I know I'm not crazy. I know what I see, Star. Don't play with me Ms. StarDick."

"Well, actually, I have news about Tabby, but nothing like your romantic overblown speculation, Terry."

"Over blow my ass. Don't play with me Tabby."

"Blow your ass? Eeew! Okay, seriously. I need to talk to you about something."

"I'm listening, honey."

"Tabby needs help and I think you can provide some, my friend."

I told Terry everything I knew to bring him up to date. Poor Tab. Fuck, fuck, fuck, fuck Bobbie! It's not going down like you think it is Bobbie.

Time seemed to pass quickly. Three hours later, Terry and I were doing the hugs and kisses, making plans for the next stage of The Royal Fuck, as we were calling it.

Fatigue was setting in, so I headed home for a nap. No messages and no voicemails. Yay. I grabbed some Gatorade out of the fridge and nestled on the sofa with a cozy cover. I wasn't in the mood for any TV, so I lay in silence, with the sounds around me.

My mind drifted to Tabby constantly telling me that she felt safe with Bobbie, who is cheating. Next, I saw me getting kicked out of our home for reasons unknown, to find out Tabby thought I was cheating, and I was not cheating.

Life has a lot of curveballs, be careful which one you catch. All I could think of for the next few minutes was how Tabby and I broke up over a lie. We have no reason to be apart.

But this 'together' cannot be now, for sure. I have to be strong enough not to get mixed in her situation with Bobbie in that way. I feel okay helping her protect her interests but I am not going to get into an intimate relationship with her. I love her too much to take her that way. I want Tabby when she wants to taste the mix of our attraction.

I want to see her chest rise with anticipation for me. I want to see her smoky bedroom eyes roam me freely. I want to see her lips part as they imagine my tongue parting them for play. I want to feel her shiver as I brush by while she lingers in the surrender. Then, I will know it's time to mix our flesh in this attraction.

For some reason, I am feeling very cozy tonight. It must be the amazing weather out there. What a remarkably beautiful day. Well, they are all beautiful, it is us that enjoy them or not. Sleep was seducing me and I succumbed.

FORTY-TWO - TABBY

"Hey sweetness. Do you have a minute?"

"Anything for you Tabby. What's up?"

"My attorney suggested another mumbo-jumbo document to make sure you want for nothing should something happen to me. Another form saying I love you and showing you future sustenance. Kiss me and sign.

'Sure baby." Bobbie was easy.

"Aah, speaking of paperwork, that reminds me I need to call Richard later. I need to let him know we hit a snag in the process."

"Sorry to hear that baby. What's wrong?"

Bobbie signed without hesitation. I thought, who's the bitch now?

"Aah, don't worry about that stuff sweet Bobbie, you know business blah. Come over here and worry about me."

"Mmm, Mmm, Mmm. Now we are talking my language."

Bobbie came over and I whacked it on her. I was careful not to come in contact with her fluids. I was also happy to test negative for STDs after finding out that she is slutting around. I had to be positively sure nothing *slipped through the cracks.*

I gave Bobbie what she was used to getting in bed, at least from me. I was willing to sleep with her, kiss her, whatever it took to maintain a look of innocence.

I can only imagine what Bobbie could have been thinking. Perhaps she thought of this 'Richie' or someone else she might also be banging. She didn't stop at one so why stop at two mates and lies? Why lie? I hate that! Just let me know what I am working with so I can decide if I want to be a part of it.

Well, she could be faking everything. And if she was, God help her for being able to lie so long. At that moment I realized, I too, was tipping out. I was just doing it in my mind instead of with my ass as Bobbie was doing with Richie.

I thought of all of the things we had done as an intimate couple, wondering if she was always a cheater, if this was the first person she cheated with, how long she had been cheating. My mind raced itself for answers as I gave her some pussy.

When Bobbie *thought* I was content, she nestled on my arm and quickly fell asleep. I could not turn off my brain.

I lay awake thinking of the plan to protect myself from anything shady that might be going on. Why Richie? I find that quite odd – my wife and my business partner. One can't help but think of a shakedown of sorts. Well, if I never believed this could happen when I saw those stupid Lifetime movies, I believed it now.

I found comfort, with Bobbie blindly signing a document that made all spousal contracts between us null and void. Bobbie signed a paper to dissolve our marriage, and retract all contracts between us including wills, estate documents, beneficiary elections, and so forth. All dissolved, kaput, fuck you, shove it up your ass, and get the fuck out.

Bobbie had turned over, to cling to her pillow, some time ago, so I freely left the bed without waking her up. I still could not wrap my mind around the fact she was able to appear loving, gentle, kind, passionate, and then turn out to be a cheater. Clearly, I need to examine myself as well, to find out how I ended up in a position like this, without sensing the betrayal. How could I not see this?

Had I been thinking about Bobbie all of the time, instead of thinking about Star, maybe I would have seen Bobbie straying on me. Dammit, I let this happen. I let myself get fucked because I wasn't paying attention to my marriage. I was talking about it, and defending it, but I was not living in it, fully.

Well, I am thinking of Bobbie now. I palmed by cell phone and checked off a couple of things on my "Royal Fuck" to-do list.

You would think this turn of events, in my life, would be enough to occupy my mind, but Star always crept in. She was creeping in now.

I had an email from her. The Ghostwriter. What great timing. I have missed these notes more than I will *still* want to admit.

"I rubbed the palm of her hand with my thumb. Her skin was soft and smooth. I raked my fingers along her delicately woven fingerprints and pressed each finger. She was on her back with her legs slightly raised. I could see her pink delight, inviting me for a taste. She was squirming on the bed. I stared at her form and sighed. I moved between her legs and began to feed on one of her perky, firm nipples. I was in such a state of euphoria that I forgot where we were, right now. She arched her back and her breast pressed deeper in my mouth. I loved the taste of her flesh. I explored her warm skin and savored. I felt the press of her clitoris on my...

Ghostwriter"

She is such a fucking tease with this one. I can't believe she stopped there. I was so looking forward to reading this book. I was wet, right now.

I never stopped wanting Star before, of after, the news of Bobbie's infidelities. With my freedom just ahead, I could have her. But just because Bobbie and I were done, I didn't want Star thinking she could just wiggle her way back into my life, just like that. She did not have it like that with me.

I am not an easy piece of ass, and she knows that. I know I'm going to need some time to detoxify from this craziness in my life, and I cannot rebound with Star.

Four more weeks, and I will be free to spit at Richie and Bobbie, should I feel the urge.

I sent a quick email to Star.

"Hi Star, that is good work. It's good to see you writing again.

Tabby"

FORTY-THREE – SAM & TABBY'S MOM

"You do know if Sam finds out about this, we are dead. Oh, Right there. Shit, my cougar. Right there! Oh! Right there!"

"Mmmm. We are dead. Mmm. That's good. Shit! Do it my young stallion, deep, deep, faster, right there, Oooow, Chad, fuck me!" I whispered in is ear as he pounded inside of me. He was so good.

"Hell yea! If Sam found out about us, we would be so dead. We are so very dead. Matters are even worse since you are my mother-in-law."

"Well, I wasn't your mother-in-law when you started fucking me. You were just, what I thought was, one of her toys. And when toys come into the house, sometimes other people want to play with them. And, technically, I am not your mother-in-law since you two aren't married, yet. Now fuck me, Chad. We don't have much time."

"You are a fucking delicious cougar. You want more fuck. Here's more fuck."

He began to take faster, deeper strokes in and out of my vagina. I could not believe I lucked into this stallion. I haven't had dick like this since I can remember. I would be crazy to turn this down since I haven't been fucked in three years. Yes, my husband and I are very romantic. We hold hands, we kiss, we dance, and we cuddle. The public loves our affection. What they don't know is the fuck stops there. Well, there is no fucking; there's just lots of cuddling, dates, and kisses.

Who knew Chad's dick would get hard that day when he came by to drop off some of my kitchen pans? Who knew I would notice and not be able to stop staring? Who knew my husband would be out of town? Who knew Sam was at the movies with Tab?

Who knew we would have time to share a beer, as we sat on the same couch watching a bit of the news and chatting about nothing in particular? Who knew I would go to kiss him on the cheek as he prepared to leave, and our lips would meet?

Who knew he would be fucking me since that accidental kiss? Who knew? God, help me, I hope no one ever knows. I need to put an end to this, but it's so good!

"Oh Chad, fuck, fuck, fuck, oh yeah, fuck me good Chad. We --- don't --- have --- much --- time --- ah --- ah --- fuck --- me --- Chad --- fuck --- me!"

"Yes mami. Chad will fuck you my sweet cougar. Chad fuck you good."

"Take it!"

FORTY-FOUR - STAR

"Hey Jeff, what's up?"

"Not too much. Holding down the forte here, representing you baby girl. What you need? Who you need? Tell me."

"You are a nut, Jeff. I can't imagine the center without you."

"I know girl. I am all of that and that and that, oh and that!"

I laughed and told him to patch me through to Lexis. "Hey Lexis, how are things? Are we a go for the Turnstyle buyout?"

"Yes, Star. We are a go and we are ahead of schedule because they signed today!"

"That's excellent, Lexis. What made them sign early? I thought we were going to meet Thursday to talk once more before the decision came down."

"Honey, the decision is down, now. They said they signed early because they realized there was no reason not to sign. Can you believe they told me that? Awesome! Awesome! Awesome! We are now the proud owners of three more locations in the metro area. Just need to convert them to our signature and voila!! Can you see it? More MyBody, locations near you. Did you hear the 's' after the word location, Star?"

I chuckled with Lexis. She had a way of making business fun and I was drawn to that quality when seeking a partnership. "I heard the 's' as in us just bought some properties! Woo-hoo! Go us! Go us!"

"Yep, and I gotta go. My mom is in the lobby, waiting for me to take her to lunch. I can't have her storming the halls, talking mess, looking for some attention. You know she's crazy and you know I am not lying."

"Apples and trees, my friend. Have fun with mom. Give her a hug from me."

"Sure thing, Star. Chat later". And then she was gone.

I was happy for the news. Heck it saved me a meeting, and we expanded our assets. The timing could not have been better.

This had to be the grace of God at work. Three properties acquired, basically at the price for one just ten years ago. The recession was really taking a toll on people. I was lucky not to be one of them. MyBody was doing great. No business like the fitness business.

I wished Tabby were here to share in this moment. She was my biggest fan. I remembered when the first location was opened downtown. After Tabby and I got home from the party, Tabby took my hand as we walked through the front door. I felt her squeezing my palm just enough to let me know she was controlling the situation, yet soft enough to cause every hair on my body to shoot straight in the air. I loved the way she touched me.

She walked me toward the back of our home. We continued to walk through the back sliding doors and Tabby walked me directly into the pool, with all of our clothing still on. I followed her, feeling so carefree. Isn't that how it should always be? Free of cares, living in the present.

After we basically skipped into the pool, Tabby began to take off her clothes. I tantalized her with my eyes. I looked at her, and then I turned away and swam off.

"Oh, not interested, huh", Tabby teased. I said nothing. Instead, I submerged deeper into the water and swam toward her. I touched her between the legs and then I surfaced behind her.

I placed my hands on her shoulders and pressed by body against her. Tabby still had on some of her clothes, in particular her undergarments. I kissed the back of her neck as she sighed in delight. I could see the water begin to dance with us as the waves started to take on a pattern, rocking slowly back and forth just as we did.

I kissed the back of Tab's ears and ran my fingers just below the base of her hairline. She giggled softly, with a low tigress style.

"Mmm."

I felt Tab pull away just enough to know she was on the move. She waded toward the pool step. She removed her panties and opened her legs, while placing her hands behind her on a higher step. She still had on that killer purple bra with the lace.

I swam toward her and stopped a couple of feet away from her. I stared into her eyes and began to lick my lips. Tabby knew I was hungry for her. She motioned her hand for me to come closer. Instead, I submerged myself again and moved between her legs. I placed one finger at the opening of her vagina and lingered.

Tabby jumped. I rose between her legs and placed my lips on hers, as she parted her mouth to receive my curious tongue. I leaned in to feel her flesh on me. I never ever, ever tired of being on the giving and receiving ends of Tab's passion.

We got so wrapped into each other's bodies, that we slid off the step, and laughed. Tabby swam away to a more shallow part of the pool and stood up to look at me. I swam over to her, while never taking my eyes off of her form. I moved closer as if to kiss her, and quickly splashed water on her. She splashed back and we had an intense water fight for the next few minutes.

"You are such a nut, Star."

"I can be."

Tabby never got her bra off in the pool, and I remained in my clothes. We laughed a bit about our water fight, particularly arguing about who won the battle. After a little more laughing, I moved to get out of the pool. Tabby followed me. She took my hand, and led the way to a blissful indoor rendezvous.

I was getting so worked up, thinking about Tabby, that I felt pressed to go to her office and take her right now. I was happy when the phone rang.

FORTY-FIVE - TABBY

"Hey babe, it's Sam. You got time for a lunch with your sister and nephew."

"Wait, it's a boy?"

"I don't know for sure, but I think so."

"That's cool news."

"We can talk more about it over lunch. What say you?"

"I want to, but I can't today. I need to run by mom and dad's house for a few minutes. I have an HTML book in the basement that I want to get my hands on. It's a one of a kind as you might imagine since it's in mom's basement. Sort of antique-ish."

"And you have to do that now?"

"Actually, yes because I need to cite some materials for a presentation that I have this coming week."

"I can meet you there and we can have lunch with mom."

234 Ghostwriter · Terry Birchwood

"Actually, mom isn't home. I called and she didn't answer. I'm just gonna swing by and get the book, and then I need to go full gear for the next couple of days, nestled away from civilization."

"I am not civilization. I am your sister, Tabby, remember me?"

"Don't even try that, remember crap. If you want to have lunch in another hour or so, I can meet you, but just not right now Sam. I keep putting this off and now I am at the deadline. Once I get the book, I can at least breathe a little, knowing I have the content to finish my presentation."

"Hmmm. Let me think. Another hour. Oh shucks, I have to meet Chad in another hour for class. That won't work. Anyway, I'm hungry now. Love you. I'll call you later. Good luck with that book thing."

"Love you, too, Sam. If you don't call me, I'll call you. We need to have lunch and talk about some of the things I'm responsible for in this wedding."

"Smooches. Food calls."

I headed to mom's house. When I got there, she was home. "Mom, I called half an hour ago, where were you?"

"A little nosey, aren't we dear? I was probably in the yard, taking out the trash or something. You know I can't sit still for long."

"Oh, well I just want to get a book from the basement to prepare for a presentation I've got in a couple of days."

"A book from the basement is going to help you now?"

"Mom, you wouldn't understand. It's a coding thing."

"I don't want to. It's a me thing."

We laughed at my mom's attempt at being a diva. She even snapped her finger when she threw her version of shade.

FORTY-SIX - RICHARD

"I hope Tabby brings us good news, Henry. Remember, what's at stake. It's been a few months into this investment, and I am ready to see the return on it."

We got out of the elevator and headed to the receptionist. Tabby was already in the lobby waiting for us.

"Hi, Richard. It's good to see you. How are things? How is your father, Nicholas?"

"Tabby, the pleasure is always mine. My father is well. He sends his regards that he could not make the meeting. He has business of an extreme nature, out of the country. He hopes you will understand."

"Of course. No harm, no foul. Henry, how are you doing?"

"I am well, Tabitha. Thanks. It's good to see you, as always."

"Gentlemen, take any seat, and let's get down to business. I don't want to tie up your entire afternoon. Would anyone like a drink before we get started?"

"Water would be good."

"For me, too, thanks."

"No problem, gentlemen. I will get a coffee so I will be a couple of minutes, then we can get comfortable and get some business put away for the day. I'll be right back." Tabby left the room.

"Hey Henry. Get some photos of that paper, there, the one under the folder. I noticed Tabby push that back in place, before she left the room."

"Seriously?"

"Hurry the fuck up, Henry. Do not fuck this up. Get the damned photos."

FORTY-SEVEN - TABBY

"Are you sure you're ready for this to go down Tabby?"

"Of course I am Charles. You dare ask. We have been planning for weeks for this event. We are in an unbeatable position with that bastard."

"And Star?"

"What about Star?"

"Was she able to work out everything we need with Terry?"

"Yup, no stone is unturned, Charles. No stone. That bitch is going down. And Richie is going down with her."

"And Bobbie. Does she have a chance at anything? That bitch---"

"Charles, I don't want to get hyped thinking about Bobbie. Right now, I could beat that bitch with a bat. The only thing she has a chance at getting is the fuck out of here with the clothes on her back and whatever else she fucking came into my life with. She can take her money and smile and shove it up her own ass. I'll help her do it."

"Okay, I see what you mean. Let's not get hyped on her."

"Yea, let's not get hyped on her."

Charles and I discussed a few more things before we went on to other responsibilities. I had a few minutes before meeting with the software developer who was in charge of developing the switch program.

I checked my emails and there was her name, 'Star'. Just the sight, mention or thought of her name still produced goose bumps across my flesh. Damn!

I could feel her holding me even though she was not here right now. I felt her sitting behind me, holding my torso as I rested my head on her shoulder. I imagined her rubbing my back, like she used to, helping to relieve the tension of any given moment. I recalled how Star used to stop by my office to relieve me with those commanding hands of hers.

Hell, she relieved me in many ways. I would look at her picture on my desk, and swim off into a fantasy or memory. I used to run my finger across my favorite photograph of her making a funny face in the park.

I realized how lucky I am to have Star here for me right now, especially after dumping her without a clear explanation. I cannot figure out for the life of me why she has not taken a woman into her bed since we broke up, or so she says.

I can't be an ass again, and quickly fall for what anyone says to me. Bobbie and Star demonstrated how people could hurt you in places you don't know existed.

Just thinking of Bobbie sickened me deeply. I was starting to feel angry, so I began to breathe slowly and think about nature. Nature always has a way of settling me.

FORTY-EIGHT - BOBBIE

"So you really don't think Richard knows about this?"

"He is too damned conceited and stupid to know about anything! And besides, if he finds out, what the hell is he going to do? Huh? Tell me."

"Um, maybe hire some people to kick your face up your ass, or even, kick your ass six feet under, or sixty feet deep in the ocean, or----"

"What the fuck is with you describing ways to see me hurt or dead? Really! What the fuck is your problem?"

"Look, I know Richard is a son of a bitch and when he is not happy, everybody around him knows and feels it."

"Look Henry, if you don't want to do this, you can back out! I didn't beg your ass to make money."

"No, I am good. I'm just making sure we don't get caught."

"Like I said, if you don't want to do this, you can go. If you want to stay, you need to shut the fuck up with that paranoid shit. Are we cool?"

"We're cool, Bobbie."

Henry was so whiny. It's a wonder he made it this far, being a sleaze. I can't imagine where he found the nerves, since he was always nervous.

I did love fucking Richie, but I did not love him. There is no reason to give him half of anything. All's fair in love and war. Right? Henry, on the other hand, would be happy with a much smaller amount of the take. He was such a low roller.

Henry was in a position of trust where he could help me set up the Watsons so they would get fucked and not come after me. Henry had access to all of the shady financial paperwork that could take the Watson family down. Now that I had a copy of that paperwork, Richie and his dad should be happy to back the fuck off coming after me when they see what I know about them. Tabby was willing everything to me, not them, and I planned to keep it that way.

FORTY-NINE - LEXIS

Call me crazy, but I could swear I saw Star and Tabby having lunch. Those two always worked to stay as far away from each other as possible.

I haven't seen them together since they broke up. Well, since I broke them up.

I could tell they still had feelings for each other, but I couldn't imagine them acting on those feelings, with Tabby being married to Bobbie. Tabby was a loyal one, for sure. When she was with someone, everyone knew it.

I decided to check with Star to confirm my speculation about them.

"Hey Star, how's it going? How was your day? Anything new?"

"It was good. I just poked around town. You know me."

"I bet you poked something. I was thinking about going to Danny Boy's tonight. Have you been there yet?"

"Actually no, but I was just in the neighborhood for lunch and heard the buzz. I think they are going to do great in the neighborhood. The food in incredible."

Hmmm. She was just in the neighborhood where I thought I saw her with Tabby. I had better keep a closer eye on them. If they get back together, I may never have a chance to get with Star.

FIFTY - STAR

"She knew too much. How in the hell could she know this stuff? Nobody gets lucky and guesses this shit, Star."

"Look Tabby, I can only tell you, I did not cheat on you! I don't know who the fuck this is, but I can bet you that I will find out and bring that person to you."

"So you are going to hire someone, huh! How do I know you won't hire someone to lie for you?"

"Shit, Tabby, I don't know what to do then. I have to hope darkness is cast in light."

"Oh, I think it's already in the light. Look, I have worked so hard to get you out of my mind. I am not there yet, but it gets better each day. I can't afford to be hurt like that again. I can't go there with---"

"Wait, Tabby. I did not hurt you. I didn't cheat on you. I still love you. I don't know who wrote you that letter, or why you got it. I was not fucking another lady. I still haven't taken a mate to this day. I swear on everything that I am. I didn't cheat on you."

"Ok, I need to stop this conversation for now. This is too much. I've got to deal with this Bobbie shit first."

"Ok, ok."

"I appreciate everything you're doing to help me. I love you always for that, if nothing else."

"If nothing else?"

"Star, I can't---"

"Ok, ok, I'm sorry. Let's do this at another time. Just know I am not guilty of whatever is in that note."

"Don't be sorry. Look, I've gotta get out of here. I'm meeting Charles at Twilight to take him out for his birthday."

"Cool, wish him happy birthday for me."

"Of course. Good seeing you."

And with that, Tabby was gone. I stayed at the diner for a while. This place was a distance from our social circle so I felt comfortable going unnoticed by any one.

FIFTY-ONE - BOBBIE

"Damned daddy. You sure know how to fuck me! Damn! Damn! Damn!"

"I can't hear you. Whose pussy?"

"Yours!!!"

Richie sure could fuck, but that was not enough for me. I had no plans for splitting the kitty in half with Richie. I could retire for the rest of my life, never want for anything, watch Tabby dissolve into nothing, and feel good about it.

"Uh, I'm gonna come!!!!!!"

"Shit! Hold on Richie; that could be Tabby."

"Fuck, Tabby!"

"Actually, if it's her, I've gotta get it. I am sure your dick will still be hard when I am done. It won't take long. Shit, it's her on the phone. Dammit."

"Hey sweet Tabby. How's your day?"

"Sweetest one so far, I believe."

"Oh really, I can't make it sweeter."

"You already did. I talked with Sam about investing in your newest venture and she is going to meet us in an hour, at home, so don't be late."

"Of course I won't be late, sweet. I wouldn't miss this. I'm excited."

"See you then."

"Ok, Tabby. Kisses."

I hung up the phone and climbed back on the sofa with Richie. Before I could get comfortable, again, he was already fondling outside my pussy, looking for a way in.

"What the fuck was all that sweetie shit?"

"Come on Richie, enough already."

"Really, what's up?"

"You right now, put it up inside me."

Richie grabbed the head of his dick and guided it inside me. He pounded on my pussy until he exploded.

He liked to linger after he came. Sometimes I let him, but most of the time, I gently moved away, insisting I had little time and I did not want to get caught."

"So, what's up for the night, babe?"

"I'm working on getting Sam to invest her money in the newest restaurant. She's meeting us at the house in less than an hour. Why not take the family for a ride, too? I will destroy Tabby and her sister. Priceless. Just a few more months."

"You are a crazy bitch."

"The crazy bitch that your ass can't get enough of, Richie. Your crazy bitch."

"Hey crazy bitch. Come see what I can do for you in three minutes. That leaves you forty-five minutes to get home to wifey."

I took Richie up on his offer. I couldn't believe he could come again, so quickly, but he did, and I did, too.

"Alright stud, I need to clean up and get home. Let's get a move on."

FIFTY-TWO - BOBBIE

When I pulled up to our home, there was a huge moving truck outside. I could not believe one of our neighbors was moving, or a new one was coming, and they blocked the damned driveway and space in front of my home. I am not in the mood for this. Have to be gentle Bobbie, gentle Bobbie, gentle Bobbie.

"Hey, how's it going? Do you realize that you are blocking someone else's driveway?"

"No ma'am. We are clear of the two homes around us. The owner made sure."

"Actually, I live here and I am not moving, so I guess you made a mistake."

"I am sorry ma'am. You will have to talk to the person inside. We are just doing what she says."

"Ok, no problem, which home are you working for?"

No, fucking way! Am I at the wrong block? That son of a bitch just pointed directly to my home! I could not help but stand in awe for a moment as I saw a moving man coming from within my home. He pushed several boxes on a pulley. What the fuck is going on?

I headed inside the home and saw Tabby showing another mover how to carry some of my paintings. I could say nothing. I just stood there, looking at Tabby talk as if I were watching someone else's story. What the fuck is going on?

Tabby must have felt my presence because she said, "Hi Bobbie" without ever looking back. What is this shit?

"Hey babe. What's going on?"

"I'll be with you in a moment." She never looked around. Once she finished talking to the mover, she walked over to me, showed me the brightest smile, and said, "Hey babe, it's over. We are almost done loading your shit into the truck and then I advise you to leave."

"This is a joke. Come on Tabby, this is not funny. What is going on?"

"Actually nothing is going on anymore, fucking zilch, kaput, poof, gone, over, dead, buried, road kill."

"You can't be serious. Come on Tab, what's going on? For real."

"You've been going on, with that Richie motherfucker. I know about you and Richie. It is time to go. If you don't leave this home when that truck is completely packed, I will call the police. And by the way, we will be done in about fifteen minutes."

"Richie who? I don't know what you're talking about Tab."

"Bobbie, really, let's not go there. Let's just be adults here. I know that you know Richie and I know you are fucking him. I want you to get the fuck out. Hell, let's make it now. You can sit in the car until the movers are done and then lead that truck to your new fucking home because you don't live here anymore. Now get the fuck out."

©2010 Ghostwriter | Terry Birchwood

"You think it's going to be that easy, Tabby. You ruined my fucking life! And I am not leaving here until I ruin yours!"

"What the fuck are you talking about? I ruined your life? Bitch please, get---"

Before Tabby could finish her sentence, I lunged at her. No fucking way was she going to throw me out! No fucking way! I grabbed her by the neck, pushed her into the adjacent room, and locked the door shut behind us.

"Bitch, please, my ass! Oh, you ruined my life, you little bitch! Because of you, I lost everything! Fucking everything! It's your turn, bitch!"

I held onto Tabby's neck as I stared into her eyes. I hoped she could feel all of the hate I had for her. I wanted her to know that I was going to destroy her. A few more fucking months is all I needed, after all these fucking years! What the fuck happened? Well, it's too late now. I will just kill this bitch, in here right now, and blame it on the movers. She left me plenty of money. I don't need to wait any longer.

Tabby gasped for air. "Bitch, you'd better enjoy what little air you're getting because it is *lights* out. Remember my face the way it looks now, thanks to you. I lost my life, and it's time for you to lose yours."

FIFTY-THREE - TABBY

Bobbie choked me with both of her hands. I could not pry her hands from my neck. I kicked her between the legs, with all of my might. She released my neck to grab between her legs. I punched that crazy bitch across her left jaw. She thinks she's gonna choke me to death, and that's that! Oh, fuck no!

"What the fuck is wrong with you Bobbie? You're gonna fucking try to kill me because I found out you are cheating on me with Richard Watson! Really?"

As Bobbie bent down to get her wits about her, I punched her again, this time on the right jaw. She could not help but go down. Blood spewed from her lips, but she maintained that deranged fucking look on her face. What the fuck is going on? All this over Richie!

I turned to head to the door, but Bobbie grabbed my left leg, and I fell face down onto the floor. Thank God for carpet, but my nose hurt like hell. I felt the red liquid begin to drip from my nose. I quickly turned

259 - Ghostwriter | Terry Birchwood

on my back and kicked at Bobbie's hand until she let go of my foot. She scrambled to get up, but I pushed her on her back and leapt on top of her. Pinning down her hands, as she tried to roll back and forth to force me off her, I asked, "What the fuck is wrong with you Bobbie?"

"What's wrong? You're what's wrong bitch! Because of you and your fucking *TAB BEE* license plate, I get to ---"

"Wait, you said *TAB BEE*. How do you know about my old license plate?"

Bobbie struggled to get from beneath me, and she almost toppled me, but I held on with everything I could muster. And I held those wild fucking hands in place.

"How the fuck do I know about it? Look at these fucking scars, Tabby. You are the reason I have these scars! Get off me bitch! So help me, I am going to scar your ass up, for life!"

Bobbie pushed and I fell sideways to the floor. She reached out for my neck as I fell to the side. I could feel her nails scrape at my skin and I felt the burn in a couple of places. I closed my fist and pounded the side of her face like I was banging a gavel at court.

I hit her until she had the sense to grab my hand. We were both on our sides, holding each other's hands, struggling for freedom. I was not letting this bitch kick my ass. Oh no, not today.

"I never hurt you Bobbie. I never hurt anyone. What are you talking about?" I managed to get back on top of her and pin her down.

"Do you remember that car accident, on frat party night, when you were in college, where the girl, Melissa Owens, went into the ditch and crushed bones, burned skin, and almost died?" Bobbie spit out her words between trying to knock me off her.

"So, what the fuck has that to do with me, Bobbie? I never went to a fucking frat party in college, you crazy bitch!"

"Well you went somewhere bitch!"

"What the fuck, Bobbie? I let Sam borrow my car that night. She told me all about the party and the accident when she got home."

I struggled to talk while pinning Bobbie on the floor. It was a job holding this bitch pinned down.

"Wait how do you know all of this about my fucking past? And, who is Melissa to you?"

"You stupid bitch! I'm Melissa and, so help me, I am going to kill your ass! Get the fuck off me!"

I took a chance, let go of one of Bobbie's hands, and pounded her face again. Her mouth fell open and blood gushed from her busted eye. She knew I hit her good with the last blow as the blood began to gush.

As she reached up to touch the busted area, I got up and grabbed the bat that lay in the corner. When I turned back, Bobbie was lunging at me saying, "you had better know how to swing that bat bitch!"

And I did, I hit her smack on the head and she went down. She was knocked the fuck out. At the same time that she hit the floor, I heard a bang on the door.

"Ma'am, ma'am! Is everything okay in there? Ma'am!"

I looked at Bobbie to be sure she was still out. I, then walked over to the door, and opened it.

"Oh my God. What's going on in here?"

"Nothing to talk about. Just call the police, please. Please call the police."

The mover yelled to his team to call the police, while he continued to ask me if I was okay and what happened.

All I could say was, "She tried to kill me."

"Oh my God, ma'am."

"The police are on the way", I heard from the adjacent room.

"Good, I need you to help me tie this crazy woman up until they get here."

I looked around the room for something to secure Bobbie, or Melissa, whatever the fuck her name is. I didn't see anything. "I'll be right back. Don't let that bitch get away from here. Do *not* take your eyes off her. She is fucking crazy. Trust me."

"Ok ma'am. We got her."

FIFTY-FOUR - STAR

"Hey Tabby, Sam and I will be there in ten minutes. Did Bobbie get there yet?"

"Yea, she's here. Oh, her name is Melissa."

"What?"

"I'll explain later." And Tabby hung up.

"Sam, something weird is going on. Tabby just told me that Bobbie's name is Melissa and she'll explain later."

"Well, I don't know what that means, but I wouldn't be surprised about anything after finding out that Bobbie is doing Tab's business partner. I imagine, she will do anybody and buck anybody over. Melissa, huh. That's a killer."

"Yep, Melissa. They must be talking about some deep shi--- I mean deep stuff, right little guy."

Sam rubbed her belly. "And, we don't know if it's a boy, but it's obvious you want me to have one. He doesn't feel so little. I am ready to have this baby."

"Well, your wish is supposed to come true in a few weeks. Three or four?"

"Three! Thank God!"

Lady Gaga was on the radio. Sam and I quieted down as we rocked to the beat. I wondered what was going on at the house.

As we got closer, I saw police everywhere. Cars lined up the street.

As we neared a parking space, I saw Bobbie coming out of the house with a policeman on one side of her and a policewoman on the other side. What the fuck happened?

Bobbie had a very creepy, sour look on her face. She stared straight ahead as the police put her in a car. Tabby surfaced at the front doorway, staring at the car which held Bobbie, or whatever the fuck her name is these days.

Tabby stared at the police car, with a, sort of, defiant look on her face. She looked very, very bitter.

Sam and I were too shocked to talk. We just stared at the surroundings.

I parked, and Sam tore out of the car, toward Tabby.

"Oh my God! What happened? Are you okay? What happened Tab?

"Oh Sam. Just when I though it was too much, it, fucking, got worse. That crazy bitch tried to kill me! Can you believe she tried to kill me! I told her that I knew about Richie and told her to go. She came at me to choke the life out of me, but I fought that bitch. I wasn't going down like that, not by that bitch."

"Oh my God. I'm gonna call mom and dad and---"

"Please, don't call mom and dad, yet. I don't want them running down here, going crazy. Anyway, I have to go to the police station. Mom and dad don't need to go

2013 Ghostwriter | Terry Birchwood

there. Plus, it's late. Let me relax and pull myself together. They will find out soon enough, just like everybody else."

By now, I was already next to Sam and Tab. I placed my arm about Sam, and rubbed her back. I decided to say nothing. This was not a time for me to come to the rescue. Tab looked good except for the cut on her nose, and she was not hysterical. She fucking did good!

That fucking Bobbie is crazier than anyone could have known. Hell, I know Tabby had to be in shock.

"Hey Tab. You did good. You did good."

Tab looked at me with tears welling in her eyes. She fought for them not to drop, but one slid down her right cheek and fell to the ground. For some reason, all of us followed that tear until it splashed on the pavement.

FIFTY-FIVE - TABBY

"Who's your mommy? Goo, goo, boo, boo! Who's your mommy?

"Oh, Sam, she is so adorable! May I?"

"Of course, Tab, of course?"

"It's aunty Tabby. Hey baby. You are gonna be so spoiled. Who's my little princess? You are so beautiful!"

I played with my beautiful niece for a little while, and then I handed her back to Sam. Sam rocked her a little bit, and then placed Kara into her crib. We sat in the room and chatted about everything under the sun.

"So, how are you feeling Tabby? How does it feel getting back to work? Your first week must have been interesting after being off for six months."

"It feels good Sam. Bobbie, I mean Melissa, is going down for a long time for attempted murder. And, I am legally free of OFE. No more trials for a while. Heck, no more trials forever, if I can help it."

"Now that Kara is here and I am getting back in shape, I will get some jailers to kick Bobbie's---"

"You're a nut Sam. You don't need to end up in jail with Bobbie. That girl was a mess. I still don't understand what she thinks I have to do with her car accident."

"I know. It's freaky that she referenced your license plate from college."

"It sure was. Everybody knew that plate. "

"They sure did. We couldn't go anywhere without people knowing it was you, or me when you let me borrow it. I remember one time, mom was driving and Darryl pulled up behind her, throwing kisses, thinking it was one of us. Mom was so mad. Too funny."

"Have you heard from the Watsons?"

"Not since I sent them a copy of the recordings of Richard taking secret photos in my office, and fucking Bobbie."

"I'm sure Richard's wife wouldn't be happy to see the sex tape. Nor would his business partners want to see him snooping through other's business."

"And, when I lucked out with those papers in Bobbie's office, I knew I would be safe. They had some very shady business going."

"You handled your self in this stuff."

"I don't think about it that way. All I saw was it was either going to be them or me."

"Well, dem done for now." We laughed as Sam tried to emulate a southern drawl.

FIFTY-SIX - STAR

Tab was free.

It had been six months since I had seen her. We talked on the phone a lot, but neither one of us made a move to lay eyes on each other. We talked on the pretense of checking in to make sure all was well. We talked about the trials as they proceeded, talked about paperwork that had to be tied up, mostly things related to cleaning up after Bobbie or whatever the fuck.

I know the trial took a toll on her. I can't believe she had to go to court to testify against the woman that she thought she could trust.

She could trust me. But somebody fucked that up for me.

FIFTY-SEVEN – SAM AND TABBY'S MOM

"Look, we need to talk. I'm starting to feel some kind of way about this. With the baby, and all, I just don't feel right."

"I understand, Chad. What we are doing is not right. I am so ashamed for letting it go this long, but it's hard to let you go. You are such a delicious young man."

"Hey my cougar. You hold your own. You wear me out. Are you sure you are not twenty-five? Seriously, I need to stop this. My family needs me. As delicious as you are, I cannot lose my family, and it would tear your family apart."

"I know these things, Chad. And, I need you to be there for my daughter, and be a good father to my granddaughter."

Chad and I were lying on a hotel bed. Chad had booked the room under his name since he was staying downtown for business.

Chad and Sam decided it made no sense for him to drive almost two hours home tonight just to turn around and come back to the city in the morning. He was working on a modeling gig in the area and it was paying really well, $25,000 per day. I had some time to pay him a visit since my husband was out of town, and Sam was home with the baby.

I knew this would be the last time I enjoyed Chad's body. We had finally reached a point where we really talked about the shame connected to our passionate love affair.

While I have always known this was not to be, I convinced myself that I deserved great sex, at least for a little while. I was not too old to enjoy a man devouring my body. I was not going to leave my husband, so this was perfect. Or so I said to myself.

Plus, I love my daughter dearly. Sam didn't deserve this. What had I been doing?

"Chad, you have been such a delight in my life, and I will never forget the passion we shared. Even though what we've done could have destroyed many lives, I am glad we are deciding to end it before that happens."

"I am so happy that you understand. You know it has nothing to do with you. I don't want to be the kind of dad and husband who throws it all away without reason. You know I really love Sam."

"I know."

"But my goodness, you are so delicious. You have taught me so much about the art of lovemaking, my cougar."

"Well how about I teach you one more thing before we part, my tender stallion?"

"My sweet cougar, I am ready for one last lesson. Make it something I will remember."

And with that, I climbed on top of Chad and gave him the ride of his life. By the time we were done, he could only stare up at me with a look of sexual defeat. I put it on him, as he put it in me one last time, slow and steady, I rocked him.

FIFTY-EIGHT - TABBY

I daydreamed during the ride to The Zone. It seemed to take two minutes to get there even though I knew I had been half an hour away when getting into that cab. I was finally going to see Star. It had been about seven months. I was so afraid of what could happen between us, now that I did not have a wife as an excuse to stay away from her.

With all that had been going on, I still loved her. Through my dating, marriage, divorce, trial, her cheating. Yes, her cheating. Must not forget that. Remember that when I feel like melting into her arms. I need to make sure I go home alone.

I got to The Zone before Star, and my favorite, cozy booth was available.

Before I settled in my seat, I put the waitress to work. "Coffee please. Thanks."

The girl sitting behind me was talking at a volume where I could not help but hear her conversation.

"Hey Star. What's up?"

No way, I thought.

"Yes, I took care of the plans for the interior demolition of the building...Cool...Talk later."

I'll be damned. It was Lexis. I thought about turning around and announcing myself, but in the time that I paused to think about doing it, her guest arrived.

"Hey Lexie. Looking good, girl!"

"I know."

"I bet you do, with your conceited ass."

"I know."

"You are a mess. What's up girl?"

"I think Tabby and Star might get back together now that both of them are single.

"So?"

"I need to know what's up. You *know* I can't have that."

"Oh Lord, don't tell me, you are *still* stalking Star. Really?"

"I am not *stalking* her. She calls me most of the time. Anyway, I only call for business. I don't try to be with her anymore. I joke about it on occasion, but nothing serious."

"Nothing serious, diva, so you ruined her relationship with the love of her life. What the hell do you mean, nothing serious?"

"Hell, that was up to them to part. I just put a note out there to set the ball in motion. That's *all* I did."

I was stunned as I sat there. This is some movie shit. No way, no way, no way.

"Do you think they will ever find out that you are the Other Lady Who *Wanted* to Be Fucking Star since you never did fuck her, from what you told me."

"Oh, I fucked her plenty of times, in my fantasies. I know when I do get that ass, she is going to be just as delicious as I imagine she will be."

"I think you are imagining a little too much. You need to date."

"Whatever, Grier, whatever."

"Anyway, I did not ask to see you to talk about Star. How is your boyfriend?"

FIFTY-NINE - STAR

I was very excited about seeing Tab. I got to The Zone a couple minutes ahead of schedule. I thought I would wait for Tabby in the lobby, but I saw her nestled in a booth as I approached the counter. I also saw Lexis sitting one booth away from Tabby. Hmmm. This is weird. What are the odds? What are they up to?

"Hey Tab. Hey Lexis."

Tabby stared at me oddly, as if she was somewhere else, but she did say, "Hi Star."

Lexis, on the other hand, looked like she had seen a ghost. And, I was not that ghost. Lexis was looking at Tabby in complete shock.

"Oh, hey Tabby", Lexis nervously offered.

"Hi Other Lady Fucking Star."

Oh shit! Oh no! Wait a minute. The Other Lady Fucking Star?

©2013 Ghostwriter | Terry Birchwood

Lexis's attention shifted to me and I thought, "Well, I'll be damned! I should have known."

"Wait, it's not what you think, Star."

"Oh, I think it is Lexis."

"Oh it is" Star, Tabby piped in. "Darkness has come to light. God will always tell you what you need to know. And sometimes God will make it so you can hear what you need to know from the horse, sometimes the horse's ass."

"Lexis, I don't want to believe it is you who took me down."

"I wasn't trying to take you down, Star. I was trying to take care of you, love you, make you happy."

"That's enough for me, Lexis. There's no way you can explain why you did this."

"But I can Star."

"Oh no you can't. There is no need. What is done is done. You put a knife through my heart and it's been there for many years."

"But I tried to love you."

"You can't love me. Love doesn't do harm like you did. But don't worry, I am not going to beat your ass, ruin your reputation, or destroy anything you have. You will do that to yourself. I want to dissolve everything with you. You get half of the business because you worked your ass off for it. You walk away with that and do whatever you need to do because I will be doing me. I don't ever want to hear your voice again. Don't write, don't telegram, and don't fly messages through the not-so-friendly skies. Remove me from your mind."

I turned and looked at Tabby. She was absorbing everything.

I looked back at Lexis and asked, "Why are you still here?"

"Oow, girl! This is very scandalous!" Lexis's friend was very excited by this drama.

"Shut up, Grier!" was all Lexis could say.

"Oh no you didn't Miss Thingamajig. Don't make me finish this story. Tell her about the collage of her in your apartment and the screensavers and the Photoshop wedding picture and the freaking wedding gown getting all *dusty* up in the attic with her tuxedo and the damned placed setting at the dining table and the ---"

"SHUT UP!"

"Oh Ms. Coo-coo Cola. I will deal with you later. I am outta here. It's about time this catches up with your ass! Earth to Coo-Coo Cola! Oh never mind, I forget you're in a dead zone! Snap, snap, whatever!"

SIXTY - TABBY

"Hey, David. You look fabulous. That retro look is hot."

"Yes, it is Tabby. I have more men looking at me than ever when I wear this damned shirt. They get that YMCA twinkle in their eyes. I am scrumptious. I know."

"You are hilarious, is what you are. What have you been getting into?"

"Going through the moods girl. Not feeling much partying right now. This new job got my ass jumping through hoops. It's fucking exhausting. Once I get settled in there, though, watch out boys. Oow!"

"Watch out, now!"

"You know it."

"I do."

"So, what's up with you, diva-lish?"

"You know, chilling out after all that shit last year. I still can't believe it all happened."

"And still not dating, right? That would help you chill out, more, girl." David winked.

"Oh no. No more finding gentle women for a while. I obviously have some issues, picking Bobbie, I mean Melissa. Heck, let's just call her Crazy Bitch. I don't want to fall for a trap again. They say three is a charm."

"Well, in case you forgot, Star turned out to not be a trap. So technically, that's still only one unlucky experience, not two. And, anyway, you know how I feel about that. You two need to---"

"I know how *everybody* feels about that! Every place I turn, people are trying to hook me back up with Star. Like I can't do it myself if I want to."

"Girl, we are just looking out for you. When you were with Star---. Girl, never mind, you grown Ms. Grown Upper West Side."

"I am scared, Davie."

"I know, precious. I probably would be too. I don't know. I just know what I see when you two are together. Hell, let's get serious. With all the stuff people talk about with God is Love. If God is Love then you and Star are blocking God's work. I have never seen a couple like you two. Never, and you know Mr. Davie has seen a lot of things."

"I am trying to move forward with my life. If I go back to Star, I would---"

"Wait. Being with Star is not going back. Being with Star could be moving forward with your life. You know you love her. You know you do. Everybody knows you do. I don't know why you think we don't see it. What you believe on the surface can be the opposite of what there is, Tabby. Don't let your natural eye fool you. Don't let people tell you what to do. Think about what you feel when you are with Star, when you think about her. What does that feel like? Live in now, not the past or what could and could not happen."

"Davie, I don't know if I am ready. Since I've been on my own this past year, I've had a lot of time to think without the influences of a mate. Maybe I am not cut out to be with a woman. You know I struggled with my sexuality when I was first exploring the fact that I was drawn to a person of my same sex. Growing up in a religious home, I was taught homosexuality is the high abomination of all abominations. Maybe it is. Maybe that's why I'm having all this bad luck."

"Girl Please. You have lost your mind with that abomination nonsense. Remember, my dad is a Pastor. I've heard it all. I'm sticking to God is Love and you are blocking it."

I couldn't help but laugh, "You know you are hysterical. Well, I have been thinking. Is it love or lust? Is it my body hungering for her, kindled by associated past memories? Is it some sort of inability to let go of---?"

"Don't try that psychiatric crap with me, Tabby. You always beat around huge bushes of bullshit when you don't want to talk about something. Okay, we don't have to talk about it, but think about it."

"I am thinking about it."

2024 Ghostwriter | Terry Birchwood

SIXTY-ONE - TABBY

When I got home, I acknowledged to myself that David was right about two things. I was avoiding the topic of Star. And, I love Star.

I had no choice but love Star. She was my dynamite. Of course, I miss her. I am afraid of what we can be together, and how I might lose it again. I don't want to feel that loss again, whatever the reason, fact or fiction. It hurt like I never hurt before.

While rationalizing in my head, and relaxing on the sofa, I realized I need some sleep. I had a big day tomorrow.

SIXTY-TWO - STAR

"Just a minute."

That knock on the door would not stop. Who in the hell was knocking on my door at nine thirty at night? I finally looked through the peephole. I opened the door.

"Hey, Star."

"Hey."

For a moment, neither one of us moved an inch. We just stared at each other. Tabby took one step forward. She was drenched in rain. The raindrops pounded and splashed everywhere. It was raining so hard that it sounded like a set of drums coming alive. I took one step forward. We continued to stare into each other's eyes.

I motioned my head slightly forward, as I closed my eyes and inhaled deeply.

"It smells great out here."

"Yes, it does."

I began to back up slowly, as Tab followed me into my home. She closed the door behind her, and she leaned on the door. I turned away from her and walked through my home and opened the door leading to the backyard. Tabby followed me, a few paces behind me. We still said nothing. I walked through the door and walked over to the bench underneath my favorite tree. By the time I got from the front door to the back door, the heavy rain had already slowed down.

Tabby followed and sat next to me on the bench. The big tree kept us from most of the rain, but drops still splattered on us. Tabby and I loved the rain.

We sat in silence for a few moments longer. Tabby finally said something. "I love you."

Before I could tell myself to play it cool and to not get so excited, a grin split my face. I felt like someone took a pillow off my face. I could finally breathe again. She loves me. She said it. She loves me.

"I hope you brought dinner because I am extremely hungry." As the words were coming out of my mouth, I had already put my hand around Tab's waist. Next, I pressed my lips against hers.

A red mini skirt appeared underneath Tabby's soaked trench coat. I took her right there, fiercely and passionately. My fingers crawled up inside her coat and underneath her skirt, walking right to her golden box. I slid three of my fingers inside of her. I was not rough, but I was commanding.

When I placed my fingers inside of Tabby, she let out a soft gasp. I sat next to her on the bench and massaged her vagina. It was so warm up there. She was so silky wet. I moved my fingers in circles, back and forth, brushing her walls with each stroke.

Tabby was pushing forward and backward, up and down as she determined to ride my rhythm. She would tighten and loosen her pussy around my fingers, like a hug. I pushed in and out of her as our tongues battled in passion. I took my fingers out of her and motioned her to sit on top of me.

She sat on my lap and I secured her tightly with one hand. I placed the other hand back inside her vagina, just as quickly as I had pulled it out.

Tabby pushed back on my chest. I could smell her juices and they were very sweet. I began to fondle the corners tucked away inside of her. She responded with increased breathing, soft moans, and harder pushes against my hand. Her ass made circles on my lap as my fingers worked in and out of her. I could feel the heat from within.

I could hear the slipperiness of our affair against the steady rain, as it began to come down harder. The harder the rain, the louder Tabby moaned.

Tabby's hair brushed against my face. I was spinning in space. Without taking my hand out of Tabby, I motioned to stand up. I twisted my fingers inside her vagina as I changed position.

I popped the buttons on Tabby's coat to reveal her breasts. As I kept moving my hand inside her pussy, I began to lick one of her breasts. The nipple was already fully hard. I rubbed my teeth on it and then wrapped my tongue around it. Tabby was about to fall. Her knees buckled, but I held on to her waist tightly.

"Oh, Star! Mmmm."

Tabby started shaking and I began to move my hand in and out of her, at a fast rate. I could feel her vagina exploding with juices, and her body trembling.

"Shit, Star. Uh---"

Tabby was pounding on my fingers like she was trying to hurt them or wrestle them to the ground. I held on and continued to seek those special places inside of her. Tabby clenched her legs together and wrapped her hands tightly around my ass. She shook as she released a forceful orgasm. Her knees gave way and we went down on the grass.

We landed halfway in the rain and halfway under the tree. We both laughed and Tabby rolled fully into the rain. "Come over here and show me some of those scenes from Ghostwriter."

I crawled behind her.

Terry Birchwood uses the viewpoints of many characters to unfold an erotic thriller line. Terry takes readers on trips, involving situations some people prefer to keep in the dark. With some characters, you will feel light and romantic, others will have you feeling uncomfortable and questioning your own ties. Terry writes for people that want to read about life that is filled with unexpected twists and turns - the passion behind our decisions, juggling the heart versus the mind's desire.

Whatever happens in Terry's books, you are sure to relate to the characters. There will be times where you will laugh, cry, get angry, and even say to your self "WHAT THE ---!" Terry Birchwood's books are not recommended for people living in boxes. Terry explores many types of relationships and sexuality mixes, along with the broken and strong ties that form life's mazes. Don't say you were not warned. Just when you think you know where the stories are going, you're wrong. If you want to read powerfully entertaining content, then Terry Birchwood's books are for you.

BullhornGypsy.com

294 Ghostwriter - Terry Birchwood

www.ingramcontent.com/pod-product-compliance
Lightning Source LLC
Chambersburg PA
CBHW060539180626
46817CB00002B/643